worthy

a novel

lisa birnbaum

DZANC
BOOKS

DZANC
BOOKS

5220 Dexter Ann Arbor Rd.
Ann Arbor, MI 48103
www.dzancbooks.org

Library of Congress Cataloging-in-Publication Data

Birnbaum, Lisa, 1954-
  Worthy / Lisa Birnbaum.
     pages cm
  ISBN 978-1-938103-48-3
  I. Title.
  PS3602.I7466W68 2016
  813'.6--dc23
                                        2015033329

First US edition: May 2016
ISBN: 978-1-938103-48-3
Book design by Michelle Dotter

Printed in the United States of America

10   9   8   7   6   5   4   3   2   1

worthy

Did you ever stand up in the sunshine and practice you are a star? When I was outgrown kid, in teen ages already, I did that when sun was shining through a window, just near the desk of my father. I am looking suddenly into the lights on a big stage to sing about all my blues and pain. I introduce a very great singer who is coming to our town for once in a life. I go and come. After the bright smiles and thank-you, I start to sing. Of course, I cannot see any audience. I am blind in the band of light which came across the desk, where I am not permitted to touch the papers. I feel warm. In my mind I am the beautiful lady, and I imagine the sound of my voice is most excellent forever.

Exactly as I have taken the great bow, my father enters the doorway, and he is cross. He didn't hear my song, I suppose, and he return from his work in a nasty temper.

"Away from a desk!" he cries. Dollars from a black market in there, I know that, but I care only about my singing.

"But I haven't touch anything," I say. "You always say I do what I have not!"

And now he says what I don't forget: "When I see what you have taken, Ludmila, you are leaving this house."

I never had a good relations with my father. I never get trust, long as I live in that house.

And then, after few years past, he is dead one day, from heart attack. I didn't know he had one, a heart.

I was soon going to finish my school, here you say high school, so I didn't continue. My mother was working, so I went.... Yes, this is story of my life, what it is.

You ask why I am working here, in America, and that is long story. And why a woman who doesn't worship about men will be in a strip joint, also a crummy one, mostly sitting talking about her stupid life. Or every now and again pulling off her shirt for two or three drunk guys. Perhaps I make it worse, exaggerate, yes. You know here what is true. I only feel surprise about anyone would like to hear something of this so boring way of life.

I had one or two lovers, you know, in my earlier life. Yes, I didn't stay always at home, reading a book or sewing my dresses. At first I was good girl, even after my father send me to little old Auntie in the farm. I was angry and never sing in that farm, until I meet a boy there and rest of the story is only the usual. We are meeting in the night, and when I don't come back one night, I never can come home to the farm. I know that. Doesn't matter about the boy, who is stupid after a short time. I decide I will go to Paris, where everybody is singing in the street like Édith Piaf.

You are laughing, but I am dreaming still like a crazy kid. Someone is watching me, I imagine, in every moment. When I eat a fish at a café, a film director will be waiting to approach. He notice my pretty eyes and my long fingers when I take out the bones. Directors all around, watching. My talent to sing, that is no secret to them! The silk scarf on my throat is standing out, and my story will be told, doesn't matter what.

One day a man who sit next to me on the train is asking me if I will sing for him. I sing the American song "Is That All There Is?"—you know Peggy Lee?—and the train is a background of a drum. I sing it very slowly, and he likes that. This man is Theodore, middle age and widow. His wife, cancer in the spine. Theodore asking me to go to USA, New York. I should have choose Paris, I wonder.

Theodore is light, anyway I believe so when first we meet. He is not a dark man showing unhappiness across his eyebrow. No. He is light as breeze, and he loves a woman like she is goddess. Two things he will not tolerate only. The newspaper in the house and, second, shortage. The newspaper, a lot of reasons I will tell, but shortage can be more simple to tell. Theodore will buy ten tomatoes if I would like to eat one tomato. Never risk of a shortage!

(I go from this place to the next place in this story, I am sorry. You will have to listen, also because my English is only so good. I haven't stayed in school and only talking to guys in the bars, you know, isn't like school lessons on the grammatical. But I like to talk English to American strangers, but mostly time is running too fast for you.)

All the way on the train, Theodore is asking me to tea over at his hotel. I am not born in the same morning, so I laugh only. But when this train stops, I am on the track already to love. I cannot notice my loneliness, this is the difference, after so long. Even he is really up there, about twenty years elder, I like his wrinkles face. I know is stupid to trust immediately, but this is what I do. I go to his place right away, from that train station.

We haven't sip a cup of tea. A glass wine from France, I believe, and he kiss me with a strong mouth. Where are the angels? Here they are, in Heaven School. Never a man touch me like that, lasting one hour or more. Later, Theodore is asking me to stay little longer, over the night, and I recognize I must call the boy with my suitcase at his room. He doesn't answer, even I call several times. Next day I pass by over there to collect the suitcase. I write a short note to leave for him, what once has been a friend and liberator of the girl on Auntie's farm.

So in that summer begins for me the love story. If I remember now, I see Theodore in surprise to find me in his bed, like I fell from the skies, unbelievable. I laugh at the luck which brought me. Maybe they are stars carry me. I know nothing about love, but Theodore is elder. After many women, he will be able to estimate. He is positive is a good one and we should go to America after his business, in August.

Everything for me is ridiculous in this time. I explain to everyone my philosophy, coming from four books. I will talk to you, don't worry, about that later. Theodore recommend four novels very important I must read. We read those books together, in special order. We are absolutely serious but always laughing. Making the life is absurd, completely impossible.

So we became happy.

I arrive to America in Big Apple, New York. I see exactly what it shows in every films, so I am not surprised. The world is very big, that is one thing I recognize, is not small as they say. I am happy Theodore has his home there, and I am not afraid of the poor people. What they need I also need, so I feel only sorry if elder woman is asking with dirt hands for a few changes on the street.

I am always a street walker. I go all around when Theodore leave to his office, in the university. I discover the character, people and city even underground. Music mix in the noise from traffic, horns in the cars and trumpets play, you never know. Leaves are flying in the Central Park. I start to like New York, even I can't be in a film because my language. I wonder about some kind study, maybe return to school first for the language. It's very impossible. Theodore says no reason to work, for me. Have a strawberry, wait for me at television, he says. Even I will cook terrible Polish sausages, he mention to make me laugh. He is taking care so hard. We never talk about his wife, the house closets with still some shoes.

I find photographs once between the books, naked photographs. The wife is beautiful there, with black eyes and hair, only a silver belt. I am so angry he did that, and I start to search for the ugly thing in the photos, and there is nothing. I put it back in the bookshelf, I take it out again, I put it back. That day I am rotting old fruit, sorry and lonely.

I forget to throw out in the alley the newspaper, with that day certain politician faces on the front page he will not have in the house. I remember he argue and argue about the wars and I cannot stop him. He was shouting about why I bring the nasty newspaper that is stinking his house. Finally I am crying for all the world, everybody walking with holes in the heart, also Theodore.

Is my project to enter this world? It begins again. I cannot see in the bright light. I am cliché, perhaps you are thinking. Little girl looking for Daddy, from all her troubles begin…dreaming, still dreaming in true life. Running in her sleep off the bridge, exactly.

I want to tell you about my age, even you haven't ask. I see you looking at my eyes, hunting for the years in there. You are right—I am in one part younger, the body, and the hands and the face are adding the years. My chances are going. Soon even I can't work here in the bar, and I will have to hit the road.

I remember we are always happy saying that, I and Theodore, *now we must hit the road!*

One day you will think of me, you wonder if that dancer and singer Ludmila is dead already, but you will never find out. Possibly you will know I was a woman who try to understand her life, to have courage even while she runs. You will know the life was not over for me, that I finally have become a quite elder woman somewhere in the world. Maybe in a farm like Auntie, or maybe a woman of power, leader of people who lost the way.

You cannot stay too many years in the bar, my friend, even if you like it. One day horror movie children are surrounding you out of the smoke, and they are looking in your eyes for those years. They will guess. You have missed a boat because you feared.

When Theodore loved me, I was not afraid. He always told me I would not be forgotten. I won't forget you, he told me, when I sit beside him and expect to stay there. He knew me. Theodore understand I am going to have to prove the truth of my life, especially he knows that, and not only for me. For all the people I will meet in my life, even in this place where a woman can never think she will be remembered.

I will die in a good place, don't worry. If you think of me, imagine I am dying in a chaise longue, looking from a porch out to a garden, with my gray cat there beside. The sun is not strong, the day is beginning, and I am singing, probably, a song of lost love.

Poor Theodore never was on dry land. Something broken, I don't know if was before the wife die, or only after. A question was growing in his mind he couldn't comprehend and so he couldn't answer. He start to cry over me, lost already even I am still there, cooking his eggs in a soufflé, he couldn't see. He cried about couldn't keep me, until I pray for the power to go, even I don't want to. Everything is there—love and money, you say—and I have to go before I drown under those waters too. I suggest a doctor, he wouldn't.

I decide a vacation to Florida, if he will go. He says, you go, your skin will be pretty brown and you will wear this white Spanish bikini back in the drawer since we have gone to Jones Beach. This was a bad beach on Long Island, but for us on that Saturday, even storm clouds everywhere, we thought was Heaven. Theodore brought for us a bagel from Upper Side—on the west, this is the best shop—and we had cream cheese and bag of chips or so. I remember he told me about his mother that night, the year she was dying of also cancer, like the wife. Not the same, but the same condition, all over the body. I think he suffers about this, all the times he prefer not to talk, only to make love. I imagine our happy trip to Miami, and I talk about his skin turn a handsome brown, but he touch my hair and offer only the sad eyes to me.

So I go to Key West, from Miami on a bus quite a long way. Theodore has rent a place for one week, so I will turn brown and he will have a space. I call him one evening from my room in the warm air and he is singing "Paper Moon," when I describe him about the moon down that way. I sing him "Lush Life," about lonely drinkers, because I have almost finish a bottle wine myself, and these days I start to worry how I am drinking.

But still he isn't okay. He says I can stay a longer visit, and the check is on the way so I need to cash it. I recognize a distance grows, and all understanding between us will be lost in a short time. But I don't want to push on him, if he will need all the time in the world. I love Theodore—I see this in Florida, in rising clouds. I believe I will always love this heartbroken, kindest man.

This is harmless dress, don't you think so? I won't find trouble in this autumn clothes. But you like it? Matching my eyes, this gray color. Or is blue?

I am talking of almost twenty years past, sitting here tonight with you. And perhaps is because I notice you have experience a sad love affair, or maybe a few more. This memory can show around the eyes, underneath in the dark skin, sometimes a soft sack or a cave going behind.

This is short stop-off for me, this club. Is such a complicated story, which I try to understand myself. You will think I arrive here from Key West, but I leave Florida and return after, over the years in many places.

Thank you about the dress. I like to have it button up, even in this place. I am like in a burkah or I am topless, doesn't matter in America. The costume of freedom might be the jogger suit or the tube top, even doesn't matter, but still is obvious the feet are bound, as in China all those years ago. Doesn't change for women, only pretend to progress.

I know nobody want the emancipation speech of women, especially you don't come here to Munchees in the Boudoir for this lecture. Anybody who is coming here can study this especially without explanation.

I thought this was a restaurant, this is true, but perhaps you don't believe. After I come into this doorway, and there is no maitre d', I figure that out. And then I see a colleague, now I know her name is Annette, without all the clothes on and serving the snacks in a basket.

But, you know, is only the body. The skin, the fat, the bones, the hair, the teeth…we are animals. The body goes around all day anyway, collecting the money for the food and the warm place to put the body down for some hours when it is dark. In the light, again the body shines, moving around against the other bodies, and we show our teeth and our tits, and we are taking the dollars.

Oh I am not a nasty old woman, too wise to laugh with men. I still fall in love, quite often. I still can be foolish like a girl who wants all songs of the world only composed for her. All the sad lovers crying over Ludmila, just didn't meet her yet or lost her to another enter in the door first!

———————

On Christmas, you know, we don't dance. Leo like to be a good boss, with his great supply frozen cake and bowls of popcorn and a few cheeses. And we can sit with the customers and keep on the clothes. All the guys come in to the soup kitchen strip bar for therapy group! Leo is coming from California, you know, called over when his brother die and after he was failing in music business. Earlier we were singing today, Annette and Katherine and me, and Leo on a guitar. Did you hear?

We open up other days not for business, when Leo is fragile about the world. Is important also not to hide suffering, this is why I told him to ask the friends and regulars to the club those closed days. The guys see another guy suffering outside the TV, they can believe it. I am not in the TV world, but I feel also a lot of pain, and I tell Leo to prove these guys that. And he will do good in the world to balance what he takes from the guys. Leo understand this idea of balance, because he is lover of music and opportunity.

This is why I stay here a little longer. Longer than what, I didn't know, because I walk in after hopping out from a car at the stoplight. I wasn't coming here or anywhere—I thought, I am only going.

I wasn't going to tell about my roots. Each time I transfer to a new place, I promise to myself I will not enter with boring home story. I know is expected, but I don't need this culture card of identification. I want to ask why you haven't ask about last year of my life? Why is some early part better? Is more important what the parents decide and what happen to the little baby in their house? I believe the life story can be interpret best today and then next to best yesterday and on back, so least valuable is the first home story. I know most people will guess I am from European Union, so I offer that only, so not to anger anyone who is asking without thinking how stupid is this old information that tell about a baby many years ago.

I don't want a general story but my own story. This is not dominated by a nation. I will not feel pride about a kind of dancing or cooking or sewing a blanket that some people are performing where I was born. Why? To feel a difference from your national cooking and sewing, and then to protect and prefer my one? I cannot imagine to care about these things. I didn't come here to become an American person or to stop being European Union person. Or to carry along the name of countries like a fashion you are not allowed to stop wearing, like a miniskirt or clog shoe.

Anyway, in Key West I feel I am waiting, all the time waiting, and this makes me becoming nervous. Every day Theodore will be calling.

"How are you?" he will ask.

"I am fine," I reply. "But how are you doing?"

"Is nothing change," he will say. "I feel rotten again after last night not sleeping. During the night I wanted to call you about traveling down there, but I didn't want to wake you up. Now I don't feel so much I can travel, not this week. Or maybe I can't ever go down there."

"You don't want to try even? Why you won't try?"

"I have to sleep now, my love," he will say.

"Yes, love, you don't want to be more sick. Is important to sleep and get a very good rest. You will call me when you have waken up. Please call even in the middle of night, okay?"

"Of course I will," he says. "I am always having you in my dreams also," he says, "so we are together in anyway."

Every day it goes like that, and we are getting nowhere. I am lonesomer. I go to the bar and sit alone, sometimes talking to a man. Mostly I start to write in my notebook about what I will do, if I can wait longer or if I have to give up a pathway and turn around my life. This practices my English also, and I find this is good for calmness and patience about Theodore. He has to take off from his work this term, he explain, because he cannot correct the student papers. And he has been late for class, since he is really very tired.

This man in the bar is Greg, shortened of Gregory. We have build up a friendship, and he knows I am waiting for my lover. He is a quiet man, and quite curious about me. I argue with him about the past he is keeping asking about. The past is boring because is gone already. Only interesting is if there is result of the past of my life which matters, to me. He tries to catch me in the lie, to show I really care about my family or the country I will not say I am from. He thinks I wear a ring from my grandmother, but I only found it last week in the hotel nearby the swimming pool and try to return that. He says I certainly have to go back to the roots from where I came, and we dispute again about the self-made person. He test out the insult that I try to make a mystery of my life, to find out if I will crack open and cry about I am missing home.

Gregory is historian, so this is why he must argue about everything in the past. He is writing a book about Key West history, about the city. He is looking for the secrets everywhere. The past under the dirt. The old city under the new one. His habit is to think in this manner about people, too, because they have made the stories about the cities, and the cities about the stories. He is looking for the old city in my life, my deep dirt story. But he is a quiet man, so he is digging carefully around me, off on the side, for the old stories partway up he believes he will find.

"Maybe they are distant, but they are there," says Gregory. "Maybe they are deep in the ground."

"I don't believe in the stories, so they are not there," I answer. We laugh and have another beer.

The sunset is a time of day when the people comes out in Key West. They take a drink and go to a spot which is best for watching.

I don't care if they smile and shout with strangers because what is in the plastic cup. I go sometimes to watch the people's happiness. And hopefulness, rising up exactly when the sun is coming down to burn out. Ironic moments I like very much.

After two months, I tell Theodore not to send money. I will be all right. But he insist to send a check again, so I finally tell him I am not faithful. He said earlier, "Please don't sleep with anybody there," so I know this will make him stop sending. He cries and won't speak. And then he hang up the phone.

I don't know what I will do. I still love him, but is true, I have been staying over with Gregory now a few times. I don't deserve Theodore's money, or his love, and I will be able to work, perhaps. I don't know how to explain why I haven't wait for him. I am not a good person. I cannot stand strong when I am alone, and I drink too much and instead cry when the sun comes down.

But Theodore is calling again, and he would forgive, if only I will come back right away to New York.

"You don't miss the bagels?" he asks.

"No," I say, "nothing in that great city, only you." But I fear to go back. We are too much the same, and if the darkness pull us together down, there is no one who can help. But I pack up and go, without saying goodbye to Gregory, because there is nothing to say that he didn't already found out in his digging.

I never dream of a wedding, never hope to marry. It's not for me, I am always thinking. But when I get back to New York, Theodore is proposing it. Would I like to marry him, he asks, and because I am very tired that afternoon after the trip, I say thank you for thinking of me, which is not right to say. Really I don't know what I mean, so I tell him let's contemplate at dinner.

He smile down on me in the bed and his eyes are like a warm cake. Sweet welcome. I forget how good Theodore is looking, with still dark hair and corners on his chin.

When I wake up, he is lying next to me and look over me. He has appearance of waiting a long time but can't wait any longer.

"You know, Lude, you need anyway to get straight the immigration papers. This will take care of that, and you can do whatever you like with your life. I won't always probably be a good husband, but I can give you this. Freedom to live here now. So don't think I am going to make a prison here and keep you in for fifty years. I love you and I want to give you a gift."

"Okay," I answer. "But you are not angry for my cheating? Can we make a punishment first, before the gift?" For that, he tries to give me a spanking. We end by screaming and laughing, and I say yes about ten times to his marriage question. And thank you, even so it isn't the right answer.

This man is extraordinary, I have told you. The last thing you can expect is the first thing he will do. It is the top lesson I learn from Theodore, to carry everywhere the chance for a surprise, because there are all the other bad surprises we don't make.

March is a bad month in New York, usually, and it was worse. I bought a short dress with springtime roses pattern, and we took a surprise for ourselves in a small wedding in a judge chamber and after a Chinese dinner. For few weeks, we take a honeymoon every day in the neighborhood, and we don't pay attention to trouble. We spend hundred of dollars on a fashion hat for me, to take a picture on a new camera. We drink a vodka martini in the morning and go to the MOMA to kiss around the corners. Many evenings, the blues or jazz in a piano bar, and I am singing "Laura" or "Two for a Road" as we walk home.

Nobody came to the wedding, but we have our place in the city, and people upstairs and downstairs and on the street I believe recognize this happy newlywed married couple, never letting go the hands and looking mostly not ahead. All the world send congratulation for our love. We can find that even in the wind slapping on the back like an old uncle, fat and drunk.

Maybe I lie a little to remember. Who knows? Even I don't know certainly after these years if we had perfect love. Maybe I am kidding to myself so I don't feel more sad everything is lost. If I didn't marry Theodore, how could I be here, talking to a young person about love, right in a strip joint?

How could I do anything if Theodore hasn't teach me about power in love? Maybe is a very old idea of god, this idea of love, but if is so old I would expect more people have hear of it. Nobody seem to hear of love.

Some dreamers don't have a good marriage. They always want to find some adventures lifestyle to make the blood rush, and they don't like a slow routine of living that always continues. I think I expect this bored life, but I find a different pleasure. Can be easier to be two members, like a small club. We make a good connection about everything, and only a little disagree if Theodore is hungry and we find a shortage in the kitchen. Happens not often, so we make a good music. Yes, really, in a lot of ways, but actually he is good player of jazz piano, and many nights we make up a song. Or in the morning if I sing in the shower, he take a cue to begin a new number for us. We have no obligation to work until September, and we sing about the living is easy and fish are jumping!

Theodore look after a lady next door, elder one. His father pass on year before, and his mother since many years ago, so Mrs. Finch is little like mother for him. She is like her name, a little songbird and all of gray feathers—yes, she has been a singer! We hit off very fast, and I go over every afternoon to see she is okay for dinner, if she like to have any bread or soup at our place. Or I can bring it over. She is so happy for Theodore, because she was living there all through when the wife was sick and then pass on.

Now maybe Mrs. Finch is sick but doesn't like to say. She is so small like a skeleton, and she want nothing to eat. But probably is my cooking, I don't know.

Here in the bar, maybe we happen to forget Mrs. Finch. Maybe we don't want to believe this is our end also. She landed on that place near to me and Theodore, so we believe it. We recognize she has no value for anyone, only now us, and one day our little bones will show if someone is there. Only a short time passes in the bar, but in the apartment of Mrs. Finch it is kind of eternity can be seen. Planets are going speed of light, a year rocket past. You don't understand because it is not clock years, it is space. Einstein, I believe, explain it better, but maybe didn't figure out about Mrs. Finch, I don't know.

Leo says maybe the dancing is over now. Not because the back end of me or the front isn't pretty anymore, says Leo, but for the *dignity*. Oh, I don't understand about that, but he says maybe now is a chance for my singing career really opens up. I will start next week or on the soonest chance for a debut, and he will keep on giving a paycheck, which I mostly have been put in a bureau. I haven't anything to consume, therefore is only trouble get a ride to a bank for that, which I don't need to ask. Patrons are quite kind here, and other workers too. We are friends for the other, to get anything, of course. If I must have my own house, *then* I will have troubles, more than in my dreams.

If I talk here to a man which has interest for humans, I have great luck. If his desire has lowered, he can see the life all around, and could begin to care about the girls here. Last week came to work Annette with terrible toothache, poor one trying to dance without breath around the pole. I know she can't stay at home or even go to dental appointment before since no insurance, therefore I was giving her all tips of the night and suggest to everyone put some dollars in a cup for a new tooth, or gold cover if they don't take it out. You can see is very important to have a solidarity in the bar. Leo closed this night very early, and send Annette back home with few little drugs he had last year from a doctor. Also he raise the pay for her. Katherine and Jolie, also, because their babies' sitters and the car seat and doctor bills. Jolie has little boy who can't feel better in his stomach, I think serious condition. She would like to take a time off, so maybe I will sing in her place, if patrons will not complain.

Actually, I would read from a book by Thomas Mann, which is unbelievable funny, but Leo says isn't right for the bar, even so. I told him I would read few pages and take away the pants, then some more, and then remove a top, some more paragraphs, etcetera. Leo says, come on. But I will practice this act for him, and probably he will like it, especially when I lie down to read on the stage as I do in his bed, with those black glasses on my nose and foot in the air.

Still I love the four books of Theodore. He believe in this great book by Thomas Mann, *Confessions of Felix Krull, Confidence Man,* about the human foolishness. I want everyone to know this great novel, for Theodore. He has learned about art of trust in this work, and he pass to me this by reading and explaining this novel. To have freedom is necessary often to fool the fools, Theodore would say, but never to lose trust in people or ability to love and be loved. Or to laugh for most of what we are, all of us.

I am fortunate because my age. I would not like to be a younger woman, not today. In these days, sex isn't come easy to men, I suppose, so they are taking Viagra tablets all the time, even the younger ones. It must be they don't have passion to make love, but even so there is advertisement about it all the time and any industry make believe every guy is constant horny for the body of women. This situation could be very hard for men have to pretend to horniness, craziness for sex when they prefer to read a magazine about technology or go to the mall, which almost everyone has horniness for in these days. Or possibly they want to go to some work they care about, for instance a political work to improve the society. But isn't popular to be a serious man. Better to find a comedy personality, cover the shame of secret desire to be serious!

And for the woman is problem to understand what guys are doing. Acting horny, telling jokes, taking tablets to prepare for sex maybe they are not interested, afraid a soft penis in the bed is indicator of homosexuality. Everybody waits for the hard penis as if the latest product, carry with guarantee of technologic perfection.

This is scientific romance of twenty-first century. And everybody is snoring in the bed, even after exhibition of expensive tits and technologic dick.

Twenty years ago wasn't like that. I can't say what it was, but I prefer that. I find complicated those ideas, more even than a business corporation can understand, and no way to make money for them unless in the movies. Jolie was asking me about love, if was always big industry. She doesn't know which is love, which one is sex. And the place of money, old temple of sex. If Jolie is learning about love, she will have to take a mystic turn from the main road, which I can offer only a map.

We are married hundred of days and we have fortune of money and happiness, I believe we are in fairly tale, when Theodore push a man at his work, in committee. He pull out the chair and this devil topple out on the floor.

I didn't know about any work story, but Theodore had to tell me now. Normally he wouldn't talk about the stupid committee, which transform like infection on the mind, he says. Only I know about two or three idiots who cannot concentrate on literature, only pick a small fights on other faculty. Poor older children, doesn't make love or have a party, only sit in the play yard banging on the toys of the other children. Occasionally he will tell me about one man, skinny and fat, and now I find it is this one. He is Morris—I never know the first name, or maybe is the first name—and Theodore describe his little back and big stomach and old brown sweater that smells, because he never take home to wash it. Some days he told me this sweater smells like sour meat, another day like plastic on fire.

I find out about eleven years of enemies in next-door offices— at last in one afternoon, when Theodore call up to say now is real trouble, can I come over to put everything in a box because he will quit the job.

What happened I can't understand, because this ignorant man, this Morris, is angry about a memo, or someone didn't show a document, or the sky falling in because violations of policy in a pa-perwork. Nothing can be a mistake of humans, always is conspiracy and Morris will get to bottom, nobody will make him a fool because he will bring out some paperwork from his stinking pocket of the sweater!

This is almost last day of classes at the college, and Morris sug-gesting Theodore should do a project right away, which is not pos-sible. Morris often finding a work for someone else which he will dictate. Theodore begin to stand up in the meeting, before he un-derstands what he is doing, and he walk over to the side of Morris. Quiet voice, he says, "You must be quiet now, Morris." And all the room is quiet.

Morris look around to laugh, and when no one is laughing with him, he shout at Theodore, I don't know what. And Theodore pick up the chair and push it over. And over with the chair is all the stink-ing parts of Morris belonging anyway on the ground.

Theodore has walk out, and after ran the department head, of course also a crazy woman, and she is yelling to call police. Later, we know, Morris rise back up, like a movie monster, and say Theodore perhaps has injure him, he will see at the hospital this evening. Someone nearby says she didn't think was Theodore pushing, he only approach to see the papers, and Morris move away and then was tipping out and toppling. Another colleague agree about that, one friend of Theodore name Hector. And another cries out, "He pushed him, he strike him down!"

As every topic in the committee, nobody can agree, and each must oppose the other, absolutely.

That night, we go to a restaurant for our dinner. I don't think Theodore should give away his permanent position at the university. He is ordering wine and laughing about what a stupid backside this Morris has, when he is on the ground and his sweater falls up, and I try to make him consider about talking to department head.

"What can I say?" answer Theodore. "I push him? I didn't push him? No, I will push him again, maybe. Is part of me, now I see it, a new part beginning to show because this is a place where the good dies and the bad is born."

"Oh, baby," I say. "Now you are silly. This is from a cheap wine. Order next time a better one."

We go on that night and many nights after about what should he do. Theodore turn in the grades, lucky the classes now finish. He talk to Marguerite, this crazy department head with orange branches of hair, and is no resolution. The terrible skinny arm of Morris is not broken, only a bruise, maybe two or three. The lawyer record a statement from each faculty at the meeting, and Morris says he will press a charge on Theodore. Marguerite report this to Theodore, and the university is considered what about tenure of Theodore. Can it be lost? We don't know.

Some part of details I am not sorry I don't remember, but lawyers are making money and the story is always getting worse. If you don't know academic person, perhaps you don't understand that story, but I can promise is unbelievable true.

Morris is illegal one on this campus, we find out. He doesn't have actually doctor of philosophy diploma, even is so many years illegal professor. A big shock for the great academy! Also, a poor small girl stepping forward out from shadows. Her chance to speak is a terrible one. I know, because she is daughter of friend of Theodore and will look after Mrs. Finch when we travel in Mexico. Innocent Inez has try to keep quiet about old harasser. Inez is like a spirit of highest good, like the dove of peace. But is old story again on the news. We find out Morris require her to visit his office, which she wouldn't like to go after he is looking over her body with eyes of a wolf. At last she must pass the course, and for that Inez cooperate. But in there she must escape his hands and even the holiday kiss Morris offer to her. Can you imagine?

We don't sleep. Over weeks, we wake in the night out of dreaming, back from childhood or running over the hills to climb a mountain in the darkness. I have again a dream about a same house in a storm, with the trees cracking in the wind. I am in the bath, looking up to a broken window, but I cannot come out of the water.

If you have travel to Mexico, you know it is ancient place of mystery. Theodore suggest we go there right away, to stay until a solution.

"Xalapa is calling," says Theodore. "In the rain, we can wait for sunlight."

Is not always raining there, but we believe so. When in those years we pass through there each time is pouring rain down, with people walking as natural. There was a funeral line with horse and wagon in the rain, and Theodore has idea that always these people remembering the dead and must be very wise. He says we must find a small house to rent in Xalapa, on the hills, and we ask for Inez to sit with Mrs. Finch little bit.

When the person you love has made a mistake is a good time to be an actor. You must be for him able to pretend that it was perfect, never was anything that happened wrong. And if that doesn't work, you can say definitely it will be all right, maybe better, because of the wrong.

Perhaps you have entered the club as I did, surprise about what is inside. You see not a lot of people here, and some food is serving in baskets, and a lady is sit around here telling stories from many years past. Perhaps you take a chair for a drink order and you begin to listen, during the dance of a very young girl, probably Jolie working most of the time. She is wearing a black hat and boots of shiny leather on up to the top of the knee. Not too much more, probably a thin scarf, some white lace. Few pieces to move around to cover and discover.

Jolie is similar look to me, so one time a man ask if I am the mother. He mention the long dark hair and black eyes, and he would like a mother and a daughter dance on the stage. Now we always laugh about this, because we go ahead and seem to be success, but soon we notice that guy, Buddy we all know of year or so, head on the table and suddenly shaking until slipping over. First we are thinking he thought we are a quite good comedy team, and we start to laugh, but then Leo is walking over to check. Buddy is having maybe seizure or something with the eyes rolling back.

Few days after he returns to the bar, little mad about Leo has take him to the hospital because is normal for him, he says, and his wife like to know where he was. Big trouble over at his home still going on. We never try again this act since that day. Buddy found out we are not mother and daughter also, and he feel some insult to be tricked and show some shock because we are lying. I suppose he believe we are in the church.

Jolie is looking as a young girl, even laughing very loud that day when she forget for a moment her sick boy, Nicholas. One night, in a slow hour, she explain about her past life.

"Ludmila, this is not my place, which God knows, and he has wait patiently for me to go. But he also brings me here, I really believe, for I don't know how long, so I will develop to be a good mother to Nicholas. I must find the way for my son, so he will not turn up the same as Buddy. I understand the great mistake of his mother, I do. All her love is a waste. I can say even I never knew her, because this sorry love a mother knows."

I cannot speak as Jolie, South Carolina accent, rapid flowing along! I like to imitate, but everyone is joking about me if so. Maybe I will surprise you along the story with Jolie's special way to talk. But her life should not amuse, but only make a man or woman cry. I don't betray my friend if I pass the story to you. Really it walks without me or anyone.

"Nicholas is child of rape, Ludmila," Jolie is continuing. "I take a radical position to be truthful to my son. When he is asking about his daddy, he will learn unfortunately about war and violence, and the man who hurt me because he was damage from that experience. Perhaps Nicholas is too small boy to give him all the information about my broken life and his poor beginning of life. But I want to start him knowing, to have that advantage in the world which I will keep adding more, so he will be a strong man which doesn't kill or rape. Which refuse to take a desire for a young girl he spot in his town and transform to destruction of her potential excellent life. Nicholas will not expect to dominate or steal the right of others because the shame he is carrying. Or because he has injuries of the society he cannot self-cure.

"And I want him to have confidence in me, that I am without shame for what other people had cause. I won't carry in secret a crime, on my body, for any person. Together, I tell him, we are strong if we are true. We will only find the good love that way, in truth."

But Jolie's boy is sick, as I told before, and we don't know what can save him, if love enough is there in the world. Nicholas of curious mind and happy spirit will live in some beauty, also ugliness of disease and hate. And some portion, we will see, good fortune.

I am a quick friend to people who listens, who seems to care about how we live. Perhaps you are suspecting me if I tell you all this, and you wonder what part is true and why I talk of what is in Jolie's heart to you if I don't know yet your heart. You wonder if I am waiting to catch you, and my own heart is closed up to be stronger against you. You will see that I know how to close my heart, one by one careful stitches, but I stop that now. I am not safe, but I pretend for myself I am, so I will not harm anyone to get more safe.

But perhaps you are the trap, my listener, the one I don't expect. Perhaps you show me the way back in, take my arm and—who knows?—you take it a little bit too hard on the elbow. Because you don't have confidence, you don't trust, you put me back in the bookshelf, my category not for children. Perhaps fiction.

You have many questions, and these questions make a spider's web I sometimes stick on and must tear out from, even if my wing is lost. *What happens to Theodore? Where is mother? Where are your children? Are you criminal? Can I trust you will be here tomorrow when the club is opening?* Wait, only wait a little for answers not so quickly appearing or clearing.

Ahead is also behind—the past is in the future when we talk, you see, since there can be no other way for stories to be told. So please wait for yesterday in some case slowly to come.

In later summer we walk holes into our old shoes on the avenues of Xalapa, Theodore and I pursuing our happiness. It is forest hunting, tracking a game which is very clever in his hiding. Almost you can smell him in the rain there, which is in the mud, and which is on the shoes—but fast drying in the air. Disappearance, and like a dead-end road, sudden stops. The wet underbushes don't show the ground, so we don't know where we step, how deep is the bottom.

We stay often in a friendly café for every meals of *enchiladas* and *queso fundido* and *frijoles*, black with chop white cheese. We go back to sleep in our rabbit villa, we are calling it this. There is our bumpy bed and we fall in, with clothes on to take off inside. We keep all the warm and scatter out the wet and cold.

We make two calls to New York on every Monday, and we find out about Mrs. Finch and about Morris. Mrs. Finch like to write an opera, she says, about me and Theodore! She is missing us. Morris is like a metastasis of a worst cancer, and we hear about his new papers. We know they are falsification again, but it will take time for the review, because a committee, of course, will have to meet to protect faculty rights. Theodore is saying he will not move until final exit of Morris. And so we walk for a week more, and we collect stories in Spanish about the old Maya times down there, when a king could cut the heads off hundred enemies and put all those on top of a wall.

Little boy and girl beggars follow, because Theodore cannot say no to a children's story of hunger and sickness. We sit to draw and the children draws, too, with our pencils, and they write their names. Luz, Miguel, Jorge, Laura. But they don't write in school, they tell us, because Mother expecting money from the streets. We practice Spanish, and we start to learn the manner to influence strangers that these small children knows. Luz seem to be quite brave when she is appearing to cry. Jorge uses few words to signify his home beside the store garage, only a box from that trash place. Laura is asking only for medicine, one peso more for her sick brother, and Miguel *el enfermo* hold his stomach and wipe his nose on little cold hands. Little spiders, only naturally, invite us on their web. We draw their faces smiling, and we give them a fortune of money.

Sometime we go to a bar for evening drinks. We are becoming collaborators in our homemade theater of any moment, and we fish for interest of a nearby drinker. We create a new couple from ourselves, and we talk between them about everything they knows. Maybe the children left behind in US, or the funeral of the nasty father-in-law they are coming from, or the property in Yucatán they want to invest. The closeby listener will hear a bit or two and he is inside the conversation, on the hook but doesn't know it. This is our sport, only for fun, at first. Theodore skip into new identity as stockbroker or psychoanalyst, maybe teacher of ballroom dancing, when the listener introduce himself at last. I am in a recycle furniture business or a free-speech lawyer. Perhaps I play the tuba, and my husband is conductor of the small band on lifetime trip to Mexico. Perhaps this is our goodbye trip before divorce, after ten years marriage.

Especially we like a mystery statement that doesn't make sense after the one before, *non sequitur* calls this Theodore. Never fail to catch any ear trying to make connections.

"Please give me chance," says Theodore.

"Hubert isn't practicing any time before the trip," I respond.

"Yes, it's just as I thought. You cannot believe her, because she wants only love," respond Theodore.

"It will be 8:30, and I will take whole thing with me, I suppose," I answer tiredly. (Is that word?)

"Honor? Ridiculous!" says Theodore, appearing very angry.

Before a long time going like this, we see a perplex look beside us, and a small talk may follow. We laugh too much, sometimes we are appearing drunk.

We are odd pair, I know, but we like to play our game. Maybe we try to free the mind of Morris, so more and more we like the game, not only in the evening at the bar. Often we talk about the novels of Mann and Melville about the confidence men—these are two of those Four Books we carry—and seem we need to know something more. Why we are fascinate about confidence, we completely don't know that yet. Perhaps only I?

Sometimes in those days I think I see in Theodore a different man, or maybe two or three. I find attractive those other men inside there, and I also feel concern about where they will take us. Freedom to make new rules for life, even new lives—this is a secret path we start upon. Perhaps we can't turn back. I don't mention, only I wish we can keep on longer in Mexico. We can follow in blindness, in some way, not in religious convention but searching to be reborn, and this is a country of *milagros* like pancakes coming off the stove.

The center character in *The Confidence-Man* (this book is one by Herman Melville) is change seven or eight times his identity during the book. Is not because losing money or gaining but finding really a meaning for the self, maybe morality. All the people in the story have to understand what they can believe or cannot trust in a new circumstance, and this, I believe, is most important. I understand Theodore has more than academic concern for this, too, and he like to provide some situations for us and those people we meet, in a spontaneous play he will direct. The cast have the opportunity to give, actually so ironic, and perhaps open the heart for others. Maybe become free if Theodore's theater help to release what they hold—could be anything, but yes, could be money—and let them walk out of the cage.

Now you are suspicious, I can see. Don't get in your own cage! If we become confidence artists, are we not artists? Could we make a good art, art of good?

I like to look out a window, but here in the club we don't have windows. This is for nobody outside will peep free, and also preventing peeping out to something maybe more interesting. I imagine right here a window vista, mountains and clouds and eagle flying, maybe a standing bear in a back scene, as I look at the wall Leo never yet paint. I will paint a window for him, I think, for surprise.

Last days he is absent from the club, even he is here. Leo in his mood. Really he need the window, better a great back door. Next week he will talk, always later he would like to talk this over, and maybe he will apologize when isn't required. I watch Leo try to fit in his life here, and I know he will not. He is drifter, hoping always won't be so, but maybe will not see the destination for him while he is drifting. Leo has left a wife in California, and I don't know very much why, only that marriage was poor and short, he said, and always will make him sad to remember.

Mostly guys I have loved have a deep center. They like to be shallow and hard-bottom river, always moving, but actually they cannot touch land and one of those days stop diving for bottom.

I begin to know this when Theodore is giving up who he is. In Xalapa he make a last dive down to look around for at least old anchor to grab on. I will tell you what next happens, but I notice you are watching Rebecca, wonder about her. Mostly you guys do not see her. You have to know it is someone to clean a bathroom here—this work is for the ladies of no interest. Rebecca never has catch a man's eye, since would be only for information about what she is doing in the room. She is big one in the wrong places, and moving slow in the wrong way.

The rest here, even sometimes I, the elder one, never have the private life outside of the house garden. The most beautiful ones doesn't know any day without tracking from guys, even with a stupid cap in the morning going down for newspaper and coffee. Rebecca cannot make this money that Katherine make in one night tips, but she is more free. Rebecca can be enough forgotten to be not bothered, to be nice alone.

No, I am not saying only the usual about rights of women. I explain another idea, about luckiness of women of no interest, even society hate and fear the women who wear a flat shoe and never fixes hairdos. Rebecca is not occupied, in the mind, of her self-images. Katherine is thinking *How is my hairdo since ten minutes last when I was in the bathroom?* Annette wondering *How my butt is appearing when I am overbending in the new shorts?*

Rebecca maybe is concern about her good friend Logan in Iraq, or she want to figure out existential question, or she consider painting a portrait of Grandma, or she want to call senator about support for conservation of forest—some possibility not about her body, can you see? Can you imagine how much time Katherine apply on those several long curls? Yes, she can think about something else—Katherine is very smart—but she will concentrate first on the next hour, when Buddy appreciate the curls, say, *Baby, you the most beautiful girl in this world!* And all the first-given hours take away very many hours, the good hours of responsibility for justice and passion for ideas, also compassion for people, animals.

You are thinking, *But why Rebecca let herself go?* No, I must answer, she has let herself *be.*

All right, I shut up. I know, I will sing tonight and I must practice, take some first-given hours for responsibility of a show! If I only talk and talk here in the bar, what will you believe about me? How will you remember me?

Again we sit around for a nice glass beer. Can you know and also trust me? Can you trust enough to know me at last? This is what we both want, I believe.

So first one or two things. I came here to this bar from the car on a corner close by, you know this, with one bag. I was not for some years living with Theodore, and the three people in the car finally are so boring and terrible, I find disgusting. I cannot act for them or myself that my life is not going down a drain. This fact is too clear—I have to switch the way, even is another drain I can discover if I like more. And when we come to this part, you will see Leo's is lucky place to find.

But there is more story of Theodore first I have to tell.

I will return us to Xalapa, in rainy season. It pours out a long river of dirt and trash along the streets to make a fresh city of tomorrow. I don't know when tomorrow is, maybe eighteen years ago, in another century. The skin in those days is very, very soft and good kind of wet, and we dress up in cotton to dry a little bit, looking like two centuries ago fashions. I have white skirt mostly on with a flower shirt I remember make me feel beautiful, and Theodore is dressing in long white slack and blue or green stripes shirt, looking very handsome guy. Everything around is old wood and stone, some rattan chair or other plant, maybe palm tree fiber for a small table.

Perfect for theater, we are feeling as in old films. Is very easy to imagine anything.

Memory is sweet, and probably we are not supposed to tell those long-ago marriage stories that anyone wonder is true. But I think about the nights. Theodore close under the bed light, reading one of the Four Books to me. I have difficulty to follow, especially in Melville, but he reads again and again, and if I fall asleep, he will catch me up tomorrow. He ask like a professor if I understand what is main idea, and often I flunk out. Very slowly, very, I learn, but isn't perfect, not even until today. But I still have a pleasure from reading with Theodore those hard books.

And is big entertainment in Nabokov for us. We read again that summer two or three times *Despair*. I know—doesn't sound funny. Topic is quite serious, murder and so on, but this character Hermann is trap completely by himself, by too much belief in himself. Hermann is disconnected character without sympathy and lose the wide view, until a very bad surprise of his great mistake. I cry laughing!

"A textbook case," Theodore like to say. "Self-deception at key moment. The artist cannot be greedy or selfish, only the mark. The artist never is hurrying, always is making support, always waiting for other one to show the problem or close up a deal."

Perhaps you are thinking about who is this Theodore, and now and then consider my feelings, still a young girl, about my new husband of this short time. Do I look at this man and see a critic of finest literature, a scholar? Or someone who can be a thief, who want to carry his bride into life of crime? The pretty young wife is laughing about a storybook, and she kiss him, and the man? Where is he stepping out?

Maybe I thought was his university work but also hobby, not very usual but kind of fantastic game for us. I was full of love. If I analyze this time, I have a lot of answers and I don't know which is the most true. Maybe that one, yes. Romance.

Also, wasn't Shakespeare say *All the world is a stage?* And every man and woman will be playing more than one part, coming on the stage and going out? Are all the characters maintain a good order life? I don't think so. Some have bunch of problems, I believe. Some make a mistake or more.

After Theodore there was some. A few guys I try to turn around the world with, since I am in a broken life. A broken woman.

Here I will tell you how easy a wind blow me down then, even the story isn't complete in the other part. I run away sometimes from the strong memory, so before I come back, a little between story of another time. Little, actually not.

I am traveling, and I often find a seat companion who is a friendly man. We have the chance to make ourselves up again when we meet a stranger, and I have practice in this. Can be common behaving of a salesman, too, and some other commercial people. Some hunters in the seats, sometimes together in the same row.

I am fragile in this time, and I am each day waking up thinking I must find fix for all those misery feelings. I have always in those days think a man will be the medicine, and I take it quickly, don't look at a label how to take it without extra sickness.

Larry looks like a joker guy, getting in the seat next to me, but a good looker. His teeth I suspect just coming from the dentist, so he is smiling. I want to smile even bigger smile. Larry is going to Chicago, where I am changing. I find out he is not meeting a woman there, so I start to imagine I could skip a next flight and book into a hotel, why not, a few days. A rest and, why not, short affair. I see he take a notice to me in the first hour, and in the second hour really like to talk to me about good topics like God or politics. Even he seem to be typical American cowboy in one moment, next one he is denying God.

"I am fed up making excuses for Him, if he exist," suddenly Larry says. "He cannot run the ranch any better, I won't work for him. I am not blaming Adam and Eve for the human suffering—we heard that crazy story from Him, haven't we? If everything come from Him?"

I enjoy this, because reminds me of opinion of Melville character, or maybe is Nabokov. I think both. Now I am forgetting some of the Four Books, but not ideas there. Anyway in big flash I remember Theodore, missing so terribly, and I want to find him in Larry. On his way to convention or some commerce meeting, Larry experience a freedom quite new for him, which open up his ideas of many years ago at university. He sound little like Theodore after cocktails, if he begin to talk about a political trouble. And he is wearing the same kind shirt of pockets all over, I believe better for walking in the forest, and the same blue jeans of black.

In Chicago, I go with Larry by a taxi, but I stop off at Palmer House hotel, not where he is going, and there is a single room open. I know he will give a call, so I buy a little dark dress that evening, and on the next day we are having dinner and so on. Details are not so important as problem of imagination, combination of a memory man and a man who exist in front of me. I feel exactly connected, but I know nothing. This is a danger, very bad one, because Larry is only Larry. My heart, all those pieces, will be in that cowboy's hands.

"Woman of my dreams," very serious he says, "come to the ranch and stay long as you like with me."

I protest he is joking again, but my stupid heart is dancing. On a cane, but trying again to dance. Strange power comes and takes out Theodore, put instead Larry in all the history of love. We have always been riding on horseback on those hills. Memory is all new, how incredible strong and beautiful that I don't see.

Perhaps you say, this is best remedy, so lucky is Ludmila can fall in love and repair a heart. But time can tell only, if all injuries will cure.

Money? I once had too much, can you even believe that? Yes, more than is good, because all the work of money can be terrible. Where to put? When to give? Where it is going fast you can't see? Who is going to take more? Why it cost to keep it? Why and why isn't Heaven?

Best lesson of money will come after you have account full, and still keeps coming tears for what is not anywhere in this account, even if you want to buy any treasure in the planet. And then you even dream of a poor life. Your life, maybe on a small, beat-down road, looking like sadness you feel. But you know is foolishness, and still you like to imagine this simple life of nothing.

Money comes with Theodore, river of magic we haven't expect in those Xalapa days early on. And in all our mistakes and troubles, it doesn't stop. We came there with only faculty salary of Theodore and, of course, insurance remains of the wife, also she was not from poor family. But is not proper talk too much about the finances, I know. Everybody embarrass about money, I never know why this is true. In America is like religion competition, keep very close on hand and has more power for shaming ones on the outside. Most are outside, or maybe believes that, because no information to compare. Even rich ones are thinking, oh, I am a loser person, better I say nothing if I will show my poor pocket even less. But they like very much to show any money, so there is conflict. Can be dangerous to show other guy who is waiting to calculate if he will win.

Perhaps you consider to ask me now if I have lost all the money, or what happen, or if I still have. But I know you will be adding this to some other also forbidden questions about me. So better wait, you are thinking, because Ludmila finally says everything.

The bar will close next week, because a holiday for Leo. Also decoration and painting here, and I will keep him away, on his garden planning. This design will be for a bamboo tree wall against the neighbor, with a terrible orange poison color house of ten thousand feet, more or less. But takes fifteen or twenty years to grow so high to cover that poison view, so he likes to construct a tower over and up from his house, where now is the garden. I don't know if it can be allowed in the city, a high tower above all, so he will make this plan with architect friend Ronald. For Leo, orange may be same as red for the bulls, and he cannot tolerate outside his door each morning.

"I will change the world, here on my street," he says. "A barbarian is free to live here on my left side, and he must show a tribe color, I understand, but I have also a freedom on my land."

"Have you consider about buying a faraway house?" I ask.

"Then I give up everything," he says. "All my rights and my home, I am handing over to the barbarian and his baby barbarians, and they are multiplying, and they follow over to my new house, and process keep going until last day of time."

"Good luck on this treetop tower," I say. "Or maybe we will have lucky hurricane in September which can tear down and blow it off. Leave your house only, as you like to keep it. Despairing those barbarians and they trail away, perhaps Alaska calling."

Anyway, Rebecca will like to work on the club project with me, extra overtime money during closing time. She has good ideas for improvement, and she can work so hard without worry on cracking fingernails. She is actually fantastic person, Rebecca, with quality of kindness and humor I haven't quite see often. Not too innocent, and still kind person, this is surprise. I wonder why not she could become famous, someone like her, of very good character and sweet. Fame always land on the wrong persons, for my opinion, if you consider why Madonna, for example, or Brittany get it instead.

And Rebecca working in the toilet, and painting here and around the old bar.

All the guys will have to stay for a change at home, back to boring way of life. Maybe take a long sleep, which is best for health, and rinse the liver with fruit juice or water only, one week. And isn't anymore cigars will be allowed in this club. Better start off now to forget about that. And a snack basket will have a fry tofu or carrot when you are coming back.

But I am joking! Oh, you trust me, my foolish friend!

You see? It's all right, now you have your drink, so we now hear what Morris again is doing in New York. Such a big place, but his rubbish office take all the room in that city, anyway of the mind. They have decide the certificate of Morris is not a best one, but regarding his so long experience, he may continue in this university. Theodore is devastate when department chair give him that news. First I absolutely believe he will cry in his anger. For some hours then we take a usual walk around the town, just buy the fruits and bread for the next days, as normal. He is making his mind, so when we return he telephone Marguerite to make official application for staying a hell away as long as can be possible.

When Marguerite return this call in few days, she give a compliment to good decision of Theodore. Take away this semester, she says, and we are going to see. Perhaps something else is going to happen, as often can happen, and these troubles will pass.

"Maybe Morris dies," says Theodore. I tell him never say that, but I confess now, who will not agree? The government even kill some nasty people, so why not contemplate bad luck for evil Morris?

Now we can celebrate, and we of course love to do it. I would like to go for the weekend in Mérida, not so far, and we have a friend who must go there soon to sell some antique decoration or jewelry.

Carlos is party guy with a pretty good truck, so we are on the way! Once we went there before, we keep going there or to Oaxaca, and Theodore would like to have a coffee in the old place and dinner, too. And buy those hats which always we have wanted in the store near the big market, hope we can find again. Fantastic straw, of finest white type, maybe you know it. Even so down a way in old Ybor, you don't find this type, I don't think.

We find some adventure, we expect, in a different city of Mexico. Inventors of life, every day again with a cup of *café con leche*, so easy as the sun goes up. Nomadic, says Theodore, we will be nomadic peoples for this time. What for a house is needed? Maybe only a postal box to check when we go sometimes along the way to Xalapa.

If is anyone we can help, okay. Poor or rich, might be we can offer a way to climb out for them. If we enter a hat shop, could be someone there to help. Or in a bus, if we go there to discover a person of need. We don't expect to be ones found, but how funny is it, the beginning persons discovers *us* on the road.

As I told, Carlos has taken us by a big truck, and Theodore has package a lunch, because he never like me to go in a kitchen unless emergency to open a can. Lucky for me, Theodore manage a quite good lunch. We are telling some stories to Carlos about beautiful New York, which he has never been, and we suddenly hears loud scratch below.

"Oh no," says Carlos. "Probably clutch." Or is *clatch*?

Stops the truck, and Carlos going under, also Theodore looking beside and asking what can he see. I am standing by, so a car follow in front and the man and wife are asking is a help can be given. We are talking a little bit, but they don't see the guys and they offer to call a help ahead on the road. I explain Carlos a good mechanic, I am sure. They are looking over me, and I understand they imagine I am a poor woman from far away and hasn't money. My dress is one old-fashioned and the truck is need a new paint.

They hand a big pesos bill, and I push that back. So nice they are! I can recognize that the woman would like to be kindest hero, and she is telling the husband to give again. Really, I am saying, I have some pesos in there, but she does not believe, this pretty and smiling woman in the top-down Mercedes. They would like a good memory story when they have give money to too-proud outlander girl on the road in that old blue truck. They will not tell how many pesos, but maybe suggest was more. I try another time saying no, but when I see is possible to bring more happiness to take it, I shake the soft hands and promise never will I forget such a great kindness. The car goes fast off, and they are waving out and calling about the report they will be making to gas station ahead.

I run around the truck to tell, and they have already fix it, when they take out a stick. I promise to buy a big dinner for all three, and we laugh, looking like always running behind luck, or luck behind us.

In the night, after we put away Carlos drunk in his bed, we talk about how crazy is this day on the road. I didn't want but came all that money anyway, and so it seem we can say no as way to become rich. Impossible, but maybe most possible of all ideas, because what else than this is a magic way? Look at turning rock to gold, says Theodore, kind of logic against logic to transform. Reverse of what is expecting.

Theodore remind me of great story of Felix Krull has to sign up for military service, which he wouldn't like to go. He prepare a terrible performance of having mental sickness and any disease of the body you like to mention, and insist he will be perfect soldier. This cause a health minister to refuse him absolutely, even angry about any idea of this, even laughing at him. You cannot be afraid first to oppose your desire, says Theodore, if second you will have it. You must find the nonsense direction and take it without any question.

"Is all upside down. No is yes, and double no is double yes." I know this from the Four Books, how seeing can be used for not seeing. Or how confidence comes, like a faith in god, from no sight of that, only invisible strong idea.

"Yes is a process," respond Theodore. "Anyone who is sentimental, also proud about being good, can be turn easily in a different direction. Is fascinating, don't you think? We all turn and keep turning, and mostly we don't see what is the cause."

I believe that now, don't you? Not all closed eye is blind or open eye can see.

Those days I think he is like a madman scientist, and mostly I don't take serious what latest fascination he is talking about. But I find happiness when we make our stories up and plan a theater for the day.

Second day in Mérida opens up sun shining, and by sundown we have a wonderful hat, and Carlos has sold all his jewels and old treasures and want to go. He has already the deep eyes of missing his wife and baby. We will stay a little, make acquaintance of few tourists, turn up the world and look under.

In fact, sex is too difficult. People haven't luck enough most times to do it well. If they cannot offer attention as much as to even swimming or playing musical instrument, they can hide a little, and forget why to do it. Even a person can have fear of poor sex, which turn into a disconnect idea about entertainment. People come to a club and take a look, try to understand again the purpose. For them may be a therapy, but they can get more trouble. Perhaps they see just one part, but sex isn't only for eyes, we know that, also behind and below. Is a hard project for the whole body, whole person if it will be good sex.

Usually cost many years for the body to take experience, so is very important to see where we kiss has a lines, where we stretch back the neck when we shout, and when we smile all over the face also. And if we have cry over a lover, missing or losing him, between the eyes will show in those crinkles that never let go the darkness. If we get a Botox, the history of hardest sex and best love will be lost.

I always like to remember. I wouldn't like anyone imagine I never had some love affairs that leave a beauty mark. The skin of any person will be beautiful if it is trace all over by expression of love, I believe.

When the club open back up again yesterday, we have made a progress, haven't we? You can notice every clean table and floor, but most is the walls we have paint with so many windows view. Rebecca has talent for painting animals, and Leo is vegetarian, so we believe he will like those cows and goats she put in the fields outside, even so is imaginary ones. He was acting very surprised, but he mention trouble to see in the usual darkness of the club. Maybe we will put some little lamp below, I offer that idea.

And we have celebrate Tiffany on her way to become professional in cheese. She has great interest in foods, and I ask her why doesn't she pursue and I keep on asking. One day she told me, I am going to a school to study about cheese, how it is made from earliest days and what is this process to preserve for ages and all of that. In Vermont, Tiffany will live on a farm to begin, and she has a friend of family who likes to help her, because she knows a way out of this dancing job is good to come fast. Tiffany is a very good dancer, so this is more important. You can see if the girls absolutely can fall in the trap, or isn't any danger.

Sometimes a girl is dancing the story of her life, and such is Tiffany. She is beautiful, but not the story, which is incest. When she dances, anyone can see is too familiar for her, around and around, kind of like old bad habit she love to give up. She glance at customers too much in his eye, especially old guys, and she does not smile. Very erotic, I believe, but this power can lock her up in that life.

No, cheese is not funny for Tiffany. Passion can be cheese or anything light up from a good reason and offer freedom from drifting around a same problem. I know you understand that, but I wonder why is cheese funny joke sometimes. I notice you laugh before you hear more about Tiffany. Probably she really like to laugh also, especially now she already is flying far away.

Pretty soon she will see a real cow out from a real window. A shocker, maybe. I will try to sing her a song tonight about moving along where she never has been before, too good to be a dream. A song could start there, in fact perhaps I am writing it. I wouldn't like other girls already forget her, and I don't want, either, so it must be a good song all remembers to sing. A ballad of a great woman but unknown, as so many.

I didn't know you was songwriter big talent, I guess you are thinking. Good luck if you want to do that for this evening!

I would say there instead exist songs woman-for-woman already I could sing. One very beautiful is "Song for Sharon," from Joni Mitchell long time ago. Maybe I will modify for Tiffany, because it tells about friendship and finding a courage to follow best way in life. Instead of opening line, *I went to Staten Island, Sharon, to buy myself a mandolin*, I could sing *I went to Ybor City, Tiffany, to buy the staff some new G-strings*…ha! Maybe could work out, I don't know. While the club is so quiet today, only me and you waiting for life to begin, maybe I will get a paper and pen.

Did you know Tiffany is gay woman? Actually is perfect job for these women, because they have a big power the men cannot touch, the power of not to care. No love worry for them. Other lesbians around the club, did you know? No, is not for me, you already know. But is normal in any strip club, and if they realize that at last, most guys imagine is quite okay for them. Ha!

Power is funny thing for any woman in the bar. More clothes are coming off, less power is lost. The guy sitting in the chair has to pay for that power he is losing keeping clothes on. Because who knows what is under the big pants, maybe not very much there. Isn't extensive. The woman has it, everyone can see, and she is not afraid if anyone will take a measure.

Maybe a woman will not care after everything is tried out.

You take my measure now, like investigator. You think I cannot be a mother? Theodore hasn't interest in children. He says they are ignorant, and too much of that already causing harm in the world.

Even you suggest this ignorance will not last forever, he find insupportable all those years we have to wait and see. Stupid ones cannot help it, he says, but you don't have to live with them.

I have imagine our family, but now it is fade away. We talk about that in Mérida, and sometimes I feel very sad to say goodbye to those children I have imagine growing up. I keep them in a country of sunshine liberty and hopes on fire, inside my heart where I can make them grow if I like to, on any day. They will never try out life, the sickness and crying and mistakes kind. Only the very green grass kind, from secret dreams.

I will tell a story maybe it isn't mine but will be close enough, could be, even part is. Or could be a dream or a film, sometimes becomes hard to know this memory for content of fact. But essence has stay in my life years and years, so this question is foolish of who own completely one experience, like a property. A child in this story is lost for someone, but lives somewhere not lost at all. Is that a lost child anyone can cry about? If so, what thing is not tragedy? Everything will be let go, but goes somewhere for a different chance. Memory will carry the pain, but will drop all that in the grave.

There is a child with my eyes. Not from Theodore.

I cannot. I thought, but isn't the right day. Too much noise today in the bar, too many people. Next time when you ask, yes. Today, another story.

Theodore, I like to remember, often quote, "You cannot cheat an honest man." This is great truth. The honest man will give to you, offer mostly, and he never want to take away for nothing what you value. So you have no possibility to hook him. He is free, and he will trust, but only become more secure. And he save himself a lot of trouble, also, because distrust always will consume time. We meet those good guys sometimes, more frequent than you imagine, and once on a ship, we learn important lesson.

Travel, the way to escape any complication, the chance to change again the costume and the story. We love travel. We love transformation, I and Theodore. We make ourselves younger every time we write a new story. We start up once more and only time will be cheated. For this I always forgive a liar, that person who want to feel he is only at the beginning, young again. A lie can destroy time, don't you agree? If you say you were not here today, you go back to earlier moment and take a new day. Or you can have two days, if you like, and it will not make you older!

You must try sometimes to lie a little, I am serious—this is only true Fountain of Youth.

Where have I been going? Oh, yes, we are back in Xalapa, after in Mérida kind of lost our virginity on the roadside, and we decide maybe a little bit too much rain and funeral for now. Even we are together, we start to feel alone. We want to find a companion who is also on the road, someone wanting to see how he is looking in a new adventure. And we find one like that, and take up a same hotel with him in Chetumal, on the way south. I notice Daniel leaving the bus, when we arrive in the town station, very strong impression. The body like a song you try to hear louder, closer up. Harmonic form.

We introduce in the verandah, having Bohemia beer, so I explain I am descendent of Ludmila, tenth-century princess of Bohemia. And Theodore explain he is coming from a long line also, of guys who like to drink beer, straight to this bar. And Daniel says he is from Mexico City, and his family is mix of Portuguese and French and Mexican, all kind of mix-up blood and crazy. He is *encantado* to meet real princess, he says, and he can see I am worthy of this name Ludmila. He begin to call me Worthy, or sometimes Princess. At once we know this will be a great friend, that always invent a reason to laugh and give a new name to anything.

Daniel has family he wish to abandon, most of all Dad, except the money for his travels away from them. He would like to satisfy pretense of the parents so they will leave him alone about his future, especially they want him to marry very well and soon. He has romantic imagination to cross the world alone, place to place voyager for many years. When we are young, we like to be alone in a romantic imagination, don't we, but when we are older and sit by ourself, we feel the life closing down. Is not pleasure to be a loner without understanding, even with eyes deeper and sexy. But Daniel is very young, as I was, also, and handsome to the young princesses like to me.

But I am married lady, of course, on a different journey.

Maybe we can help Daniel, but yet we don't know how. We all have wonderful time and go every place together the next days, and finally our plan is keep going south to Guatemala and to Nicaragua and Costa Rica, and just keep on. I think about Mrs. Finch, like our family, so we will have to keep her in touch. She could add on Central America to the opera she compose about us, also entrance of Daniel in Act II. A song everyone want to sing along, this is Daniel.

One night, it is too late for me to keep drinking, so I return to the room. That night, Theodore offer his bride to Daniel. Of course not as lover! No, if Daniel will take me home as his princess of Bohemia, just for a wedding, he can after be free. At first, Daniel is afraid, but they form a plan, and they decide to divide in half the cash wedding gifts in Corsica, where Napoleon has been born, you know, at a honeymoon. Daniel has in Corsica good friend with sea cottage, and there we can stay till going on, in a separate way. This remind Theodore of Felix Krull in his arrangement with Marquis de Venosta, the great part of the novel when Felix Krull pretend to travel the world as the Marquis so he can stay in Paris with his lover Zaza, against the parents' wish. The great books give a good advice.

Next day, Theodore give me warning for this idea Daniel will ask me about, only to say might be worth to discuss. We have a lunch I don't remember anything, only Daniel asking if I would stand one kiss from him, before many people in Mexico City church. Then he laughs and both the guys say, listen to this, will be good for all. How can I be twice married, I ask, and will his parents ask about my parents? A lot of questions to answer, but I don't find objection to kiss Daniel. First step we are clearing.

Many weeks I don't go out from the club now, just staying here with Leo in his upper rooms. I avoid to shop since I have been robbed. That was a lesson two years ago. If I am reaching to get more, I will lose what I already have. I was shopping one day in a store to buy more fashion clothing I don't need, from other side of earth places probably Bangladesh or Turkey, having foreign experience. Exotic experience of taking off the clothes in a strange room, putting my body in a package fabric I do not own, finding myself to be a new person in the mirror, of course I hope. I left a bag just for a moment so I can bring another piece to try, smaller fitting, and the bag disappears.

I was not alone in my fantasy privacy. Somebody on the sly nearby, always might be. Distance is a dream of power—and is the most impossible, mostly luck to stay out of harm ready for you. I can't keep my distance, I know that, but possibly I could stop running around in many circles for nothing.

But I like to be here, anyway, waiting for the first—always you—to arrive over here before lunch, just to talk and have little drink from Leo's supply or a later coffee. To think a short time each day before the sun passes down over us asking the question, now what are you doing in your darkness? Anything has added up according to destiny? Are you more a fool for taking grab at what cannot be added? Of course.

If you have idea you are fantastic person, that will go in middle ages. You meet the bad person you can be, many times and again. But as a kid you can be stupid and you feel good, you laugh on a higher note. In older years the note normally is dropping lower. In Mexico, we are so high we break a glass with laughter. Theodore is staying young by us, he is keeping a transfusion going so he loses ten or so years of age. I have my husband and my fiancé with me, always both gallant, a quite perfect time before I will become a bigamist. This sound criminal, I know, but that crime is not serious for us, as both will know everything and will not until death share me as wife. Only a trick of office paperwork, which a friend of Daniel can arrange without question.

We laugh at the law, but what about the rest? We want to have a good purpose, serving a right and best result not just for us. Daniel is a player, truth is told, anyway a special guy to us, but seems maybe we cross a line to cheat all those people at the wedding. His life has been all good luck and a rose on top—except a conflict with his brother, I don't remember this name but has disgrace the family and put a high expectation on the younger brother Daniel, like a cage over him. He cannot fly out on short wings, cut by Dad to fit exactly inside, and his growing is all from fantasy. Also finest private education, and that has invite him to see the world.

We believe Daniel still should have the chance his brother has blow away, but how strong motive is this? We don't have responsibility so great we must act by stealing from that family and all their friends. How to turn around now? Should we participate in that but refuse wedding gift money? Risk and trouble, what is worth to do that for our fantastic friend? If he insist to give some money to us, like reward you can say, is only polite or proper we say thank you?

Oh those fools that we were becoming, and something we are letting go we love really to let go. Falling slowly down can feel like you are rising. Like a child spinning and laughing until sick, he goes back to balance only when he must.

Daniel says, "I must have your glad assurance. My essential happiness depend upon if you want to help me." This strong comment is reminder of statement from Louis de Venosta, as he and Felix Krull make agreement, so on that force we float down. The force of literature and love is not all—also there is belief that we have power to design a future, which we will own it, and nobody like a Morris or a wicked father, like my one or that dad of Daniel, will drive the life.

Honor might be a silk scarf that blowing wind takes, before we have notice it is flying even. Later we may recognize that favorite scarf, sticking on a tree branch hard to reach, and torn to some ribbon.

For small change today of channel, I present a good topic of newsblasting—this I call information rubbish that doesn't stop—and the best story was latest on those dinosaurs. You didn't hear? The scientists tell us today that many dinosaurs we know, maybe thirty percent or so, are same type but younger ones. So the young one is looking absolutely different, or we don't understand very clear about bones or dinosaurs or science—which can it be?

One thing grows to become a next thing, but sometimes no trace of connection can be found in the dirt. Mostly we don't need to know, for example, if I am the same species as my mother. And dinosaur girl didn't want to know if bigger one is Mama or another category of dinosaur. No mistake could happen, I am sure, in present time—or maybe very stupid dinosaur doesn't know either?—but I guess could be small and large bones of the past are showing no relation until, hundred of years after in the lab, one scientist see from certain angle in certain light there is similarity. Family connection can be seen in the little bump in that dinosaur girl bone here in the wrong case, maybe someone was wiping dust and place there by accident.

Or maybe new discovery is also wrong, or first diagnosis was right. Time will offer only question after question.

Don't forget about the dinosaur girl. Scientist is smarter but doesn't know answers she even wouldn't have to ask. Time is keeping covered the tracks of that dinosaur girl, don't you think?

Perhaps I look like different species from young ladies here at Boudoir. They have a cell on the ear when they are not dancing or cleaning around. They look taller from the heels, and of course breast are bigger, enhance sometimes but could fool a scientist, I'm pretty sure. Few hairs, too, anywhere but on the head, from Brazilian services which now I cancel last months.

Political problems we are having, Leo and me, some club policy disagreement. I like to have a good look for Leo, if he likes that very much, but not for the fatso trucker who drop in here. So these days now I am club storyteller, friend of all dancers, afternoon singer, and lover of Leo, when he has not mistake me for opponent. I believe we can offer fun and art and music—in sexy way, in happy spirit, not for degradation.

Our newer sign, I want to tell you, will be finish next week and install on the road. You will like it because that image of librarian girl that attract you to come in, that will be more bright now and where the shirt buttons open is little bigger and more shadow. The table has a part baguette and basket of cheeses on, and glass of wine, kind of French idea of café where a guy can talk to a sexy girl about meaning of life, perhaps. I suggest we now require a club membership, but Leo is concern about finance always.

"We cannot get too far above the neighbors or we have to move to fashionable street in Ybor and high expense of doing business," Leo says.

He says this entertainment has not so much creative possibility, and best to stay on basics, but I disagree absolutely.

"Ancient business," he says. "Don't try to change custom of many centuries."

"Evolution or extinction," I say. Like the dinosaurs—on my mind today. We have to develop for sake of change, to risk for sake of danger. Maybe it's a small procedure improvement in a business for Leo, but it would do good for his blood, I believe.

"Crusader," Leo says, "you want to change the world. Upgrade here isn't required. Guys want just the pleasure, without ironic influence, thank you so much."

Swindle. This is word I heard about this time in Mexico and didn't like it. One word Theodore prefer is *sting*, because sound like just little problem for a short time, like from the bees you have walk into when you are trying to go somewhere stupid, maybe discover a box of gold. I like most if there is *art*, like *art of confidence*, or something funny, maybe best one is *fleece*, like we are doing to the sheep and they don't know what happened. Theodore always would like to discuss the language, as professor will do, and we return to the Four Books to enjoy some good stories of traps waiting for anybody who is not aware or who want to go where he shouldn't. Hermann, in Nabokov's book, talks about a *small folding theater* he always has carry around with him. We have our one now which is ready to go when we reach Mexico City, and has stock of dresses for the main role of Katarina but not yet a white wedding gown. Theodore is playing part of my American uncle, Herman Miller, by chance nearby in San Diego, on the way soon to give away his niece because rest of family is very old or dead and cannot travel away from Old Country.

I talk to Uncle Herman and for him I am Katarina, as we make enough confidence to gain more. We tell this new life story together over next weeks as we make the transfer from Xalapa to Mexico City, but we stay very simple about facts because Katarina must be quite hurt by many questions about the lost family. Daniel take the trip home, to break news of Katarina is coming, and to say he intend for hand of marriage, if Dad and Mother will agree. They definitely are going to love Katarina, she will be inheritor of Uncle Herman, who has a great wealth only doesn't show it around. Also waiting for bone transplant, having fatal disease, even he looks pretty good. Fortunate he is trim elder guy, but won't survive for celebrate Christmas, doctor says, and wants only Katarina settle up with a good husband before.

Nice to take holiday off from the self, give a rest of the old voice and those worn-out stories of a life. Katarina is a fresh soul, beautiful one for me to wear, and I like to have it more than a new excellent leather boots.

More good than harm, I am thinking. This story we write each day is to liberate us. We write a play we live inside, artists and actors and agitators. We don't sit and follow rules coming out from the TV world, what you must eat and what you should buy immediately. What is terrible and what is funny. Where is danger, where is safety. We figure out the best world for us and how should we make it, and we make it right now.

Most people give just because is wanted something. They spend a life only answering, so they wonder why at last they have given it all for that, to explain why they do everything. They never understand, but always explain. For my opinion, there are too many good people, trying to never disappoint or cause a frustration. Losers they are going to be, prisoners building the prison. Walls are very strong, good job on the walls!

Maybe I get an idea we are teachers also. How can we offer a lesson about a different way? We believe in stopping a crazy waste of life, but can you show how to do it in a hard lesson? To recognize his own convention, a man perhaps must give away a piece of that wall, so he can look out and also back in. But he must give it—the wall piece cannot be taken—exactly when he wants to most keep it. Maybe he will try to explain, and nothing is fixed.

Then only he will make a resistance. A high tower can go up over his house.

All right, so we are looking over all shops for that perfect dress for the wedding, a quite different dress than my roses pattern one for Theodore, for my sudden extra matrimony. Daniel is return home, where he hated to go. He tells Dad I am taking care for Uncle Herman, and he hasn't doubt everyone will be crazy over fancy fiancée coming soon to meet all the family. In those days we never telephone all day, so we expect a letter at post office back in Chetumal after one week. Finally when two weeks are passing—also we didn't find a dress yet and this becomes obsession for Theodore, romance in his heart also for this bride Katarina—Daniel at last is there, in that Old Town hotel where we have met, with the same gown from his grandmother and mother, for fitting at dressmaker shop.

Of course the dress is saying everything, so there wasn't need of any letter. And this old lace dress is so beautiful I feel pain for that mother I haven't yet meet and will not know. I will not have a grandchild of her dreams. I already can imagine to leave there in a closet the dress for that coming-up bride of Daniel, another one many years from now, when he is ready for real love in a real marriage. She also can fit, as I do, on the first try like in a magic mirror.

We all look in the mirror, that night standing three of us quite early prepared for the priest, and we begin to laugh because we know it will be easy. And the dress, too, when I take some steps, all the underskirts are laughing, *ha ha, ha ha*, and I dance a little with Daniel and then Theodore, and again Daniel.

Just ahead four months, and quite a lot arrangements, but is our luck the mother of Daniel is that *going going* kind of lady. I write a letter to explain I must stay beside my uncle in therapy for his cancer until he will be able to travel and summer season is behind, because terrible for sick person is that weather down there. But actually we go to New York, where we have concern about Mrs. Finch. No word coming from her in these last weeks.

Life is a game of music and chairs. Every time is possible you will find a place missing when you stop and turn around. The broken song will show up a chair taken out from the circle. One day it will be your chair you need to sit, and everyone else can sit and after music starts again goes back to normal, but not for you.

Back in New York we knock, even it is so late as we arrive, on her door. I want to go in, but Theodore says, let us wait until morning. I wish now I could wait all my life. Next day we enter with our key she has given us, and Mrs. Finch isn't in the whole place. On the couch usually she is sitting with her books from Theodore, trying to read but many times only snoring very quiet, white head over on the side. I can see her now, so many years past, by the lamp, sometimes playing Beethoven symphony or old Mississippi blues singer, maybe Robert Johnson.

There wasn't any music. My chair is gone. So I am running down to find out from the super who manage this building. Usually he knows everything, even what you hide and you don't see him. Mrs. Finch has been screaming in the night last week, he told us, and woke up a few neighbors, and even he ran to find out what is going on. *Help me*, she was screaming, but didn't say what or why, completely mad, over and over repeating *Help me!* or continuing without words yelling, I suppose like a cat.

This couldn't be possible for Mrs. Finch, nobody ever sees this. So they have call the ambulance, and they have taken her away. I believe they would have to put under sedation since nothing to do if a person will not stop screaming in the night. The super said still they could not discover anything in the hospital, but they are making some tests, like a scan because she looks terrible and doesn't weigh anything.

The super sent a letter to us when after that she got the fever, very high one, but of course we already were coming home without knowing. And now he says she is at Intensive Care for some days, might even be damage on the brain, because she hasn't return to normal. Super is glad to see us, since they are asking him some questions he hasn't answers to give, about her papers and family and so on.

We must go over. Maybe we have miss the chance to save our friend, so we feel quite sick in our hearts. Why did we ever go, I cry, and Theodore says we should not go ever back to Mexico.

You know what is hospital like, even visitors feel they have disease and going down fast. What kind air is this, and light? When we enter the room where she is lying on a high-up bed, she appear as if dead. Our friend, with skin of very old book, drying-out pages.

"Mrs. Finch!" I cry. "We are here to take care of you. Now you will get well!" Her face begins softly to transform, but not quite reaches a smile. Good, I think, she hears me, at least that. I try to think what song to sing for her, but I can't find any music.

We sit all day at the bed. We meet the doctors. We understand the case is most likely to be hopeless.

Theodore talks to her about Mexico, how rainy is the beautiful town of Xalapa. I tell her we have a wonderful friend who keep us down there too long, but I don't say more about Daniel. I bring out little packet of coffee we love from Mérida, so she can smell that. I take her hand and put on her finger a gold ring we brought with a tiny cage on top for imaginary bird we love so much to live in there. She keep her eyes closed but isn't sleeping, just a little crying.

Maybe you have had sick old relation, could be mother like Mrs. Finch has been for us, you have visit in the intensive unit, and you went in there with a yellow mask. She doesn't know who you are before you speak, and then you know you must keep on speaking so connection isn't broken for poor one on so many medicines but, even so, they don't keep out the fear. A few times she try to escape from tubes going inside her face and thin blue arm, and we must force back her fragile body, when we don't know if really is best.

Every sickness has mystery, a plan already going and doesn't need us, and moves too fast to figure out what will be next.

Did we guard each side all through the night? No, we did not stay, and we lost all that treasure of life. I won't talk more about her, you understand, even if her story never will stop for me. You see I wear that Mexican ring all these years so she will hold onto me. You see this golden cage has entrance for sky, but the wide band has keep me on a hard ground.

We take what is left. Too much, so we give away, most for charity. What feels good. Anyway we haven't live on love after. Well, maybe we can say it is love, those bank accounts Mrs. Finch dedicate to us in her last will.

Maybe you have experience some sickness journey, but like strange case of happiness, my kind listener. Infection is like love affair, I believe, or deep friendship. At the end might be darkness, but to go there is beautiful color and a great fever. Probably melody you won't forget. And you are not alone.

We enter somebody like hantavirus so they can understand us.

Sometimes I must come in—even if you push back invasion, try so hard to survive only as you—so you will imagine you are me, and you will know my passion and my weakness. You will not judge or have suspicion because I gave you everything. Even you haven't ask, and you prefer to refuse, especially to see my loneliness is the same as one you know, and my hope to be better is the same also.

———

How long do you think takes Leo to accept me as partner in his business? No, isn't one month or two, even. One year, and first I have to become a friend and then partner in love. Men can be slow believers. Leo is strong in this way, on his own he doesn't have to hurry and get anything, so he will sit back safe until the final chance. I almost have left, when every dancer was going down the road to another club where working conditions could be much better. At that time, I advocate for Tiffany, when she was asking only to work on two days.

"Let her go and she will come back," I told him. "Or she doesn't. So simple. Don't make a conflict about this. Just make a better club than that bigger, stupid one down the road."

"We don't have to negotiate until end of time," says Leo, "if we have one policy and they know it will not change. We can save that waste."

"Yes, we don't have to negotiate because they go straight soon to other club!"

"So how do we keep Tiffany?" he asks.

"Give her any hours she would like, even two or three or fifty, and let her change that, one week before, if she would like. Give her feeling of family here she can trust it will be fair."

"And more pay, right?"

"Of course," I say. "As much as possible, so she can maintain a life. And avoid prostitution, even slightest kind."

"Not possible for any of us," says Leo, laughing with part anger. "But we can try. We can try this, but only if you will manage."

I know this is not the best work of the world, and not the best place, but I believe people can do a good work here. All kind of occupations are similar, so you know this. But would you consider my life will now become a higher one because I keep on the clothes and manage the women who take the clothes off? I don't want to be foolish, looking anywhere for my virtue, especially here. People are all the time doing opposite, finding lack in virtue somewhere, don't you think so, and just as stupid.

Is a way to listen without position of judgment? Yes and no, and yes, and no!

You have expression here, something like, *The child is father for the man*. This means might be sometimes children are wiser, growing in a new time of history. When I leave my family behind me, back in time, I become a stronger woman. Perhaps I know I am ready to make my life. The child is most powerful in America, land of future dreams, and we can see that child after five minutes in any mall, shouting for his own way.

I want to stay in front where the future, like a train, will stop only for a moment. Mostly I didn't like to drift, like Leo.

Even so, he likes to give the orders for me. For example, he would like me to announce this week new color of mani and pedi, and on Friday I will check if everyone has it. Should be *indigo*, says Leo, and maintain without chips for two weeks. And discuss hygiene of hair and skin also, he says. I don't know what problem is, my god. Someone maybe has complain about this? A pimple on Jolie do you think, or something?

This must be for me career progress, I don't know. More power can be possible in the future with Leo, almost we could say I am mother for the man. Or mother for the woman, all of them! And still a child, because always I try to keep that power.

Friend of Daniel, Miguel, is coming to New York to arrange the new papers for us in name of Katarina. This will take time, because a new passport and birth certificate and blood test and X-ray and so on is requirement if foreign woman will marry a Mexican man. And Katarina must enter Mexico, not I.

Miguel is expert in forgery, but even better he has many colleagues in New York from way back. Daniel knows Miguel since university restoration project at the museum, and he is also a known painter, scholar of art, and so on, very talented. He likes to do a big favor for Daniel, everyone likes Daniel, but he loves also every once a year or so to do a *white paper* crime, he says, to keep up from young days of his life. He is careful to maintain, so he will never forget those roots. *De vez en cuando*, he will say, *ever so often*. You know, he suggest I try to learn some few words in Spanish, to *hablar* little bit at the wedding—*la boda*—and I am learning from him, also English!

Miguel stays at our place for couple weeks, and we stretch over many nights talking and drinking. We argue about business concept of identity, which now we are buying one from him. He has respect for history, more than I, and we discuss if truth can exist if each person has a different one. Who are we, if we can change identity or someone else will be able to steal our story? Is our name and numbers, even our face, sacred possession, or just a ticket, best one for now? He calls me Worthy, like Daniel, when we are serious.

"Look at us, Worthy," says Miguel, "speaking English all of us when only one, Theodore, has a culture of this language. Where do we land in a global culture? Here in Manhattan, where our own tongue has not very much use. It proves nothing, serves nothing. Maybe you will go to Little Italy for dinner, and there you can order a *gnocchi*. It became funny joke, like winter coat in Bermuda, like *huaraches* in Canada. Like a bad weather, you cannot stop English." Miguel, I believe, pour some more wine.

"No, English will take all peoples in, eat all the rest. We will bring our voice, our sound to improve this global language," I say. "More poetry will come, new words will come."

"Something always dies," says Theodore, "but returns like grass on the ground in the next spring. New flower patch comes up on the other side of a garden. A little different, slowly changing."

We keep on going, until we go back to talk about jazz, which we all can agree is a greatest international language, born in America, of parents came from Africa, and traveling to Europe, South America, and so on, always picking up more ideas and styles. Accents, you could say, to make the language better, quite universal.

Then we fight longer over roots, which I like to destroy and Miguel, with thousand old stories, would like to preserve. And more drinks, and later and later in the night.

What each can do for the other? What can I or you do for Bella? She says to us this morning that such big green mark on her face is from a can falling out from the cupboard. What can you say? Doesn't look like? We know your guy is no good? No, better not, but I will say tonight something to her, when we change in the back, to show she can tell truth to me. I have my own story. Yes, what above has not fall on Worthy?

I told about Larry when you first come last month. But never want to tell you more, because is bad memory. And I like to laugh if ever possible, even when sometimes we must go hunting for a joke.

Larry was guy on a plane to Chicago, you remember, and we have got crazy about each other—that deep crazy that cause you to transfer a ticket to Montana, because isn't any other place on the earth. He says he has his ranch in the Rockies, near Frenchtown, so you guess it, I imagine countryside in France, *tres charmante*. How far away and how wrong, you cannot imagine, is this place where Larry is living with his mother, and a cousin Mandy. I don't think I will like those ladies, because they are hungry for something, I can see in the first dinner, when they eat without stopping so much beef and cake! Oh my god, they make me more embarrass than if I am watching live sex show in the arcade! Larry also, but is different. His hunger is very good, because has no end for me.

We have a small house behind where they are living, quite pretty style home for a guy. And he is so proud on that kind of civilization, he made it, out in Nowhere Center. He brought furniture, artistic sofa and so on, from Chicago. Years ago, but he said he planned for me. He would like me to stay mostly there, far even from boring little Frenchtown, while he is working, and I feel content for that because is so cold in the winter outside. Definitely you can't breathe. I cook and wash. Sometimes I feel I am the maid, but don't want to think about anything, only if he will come home for long lunch. He is so strong around me, and after I have lost Theodore, you know, I don't want to move. I am like I was dead, and so happy if he will not ask me to return all the way to life.

I thought this was reasonable life, not a house made of fantastic cards, as in the past with Theodore.

Larry is like a good dog you love very much, but he is a dog who bites. You don't want to give that dog away, even if he hurt someone. Even when he hurt you.

I will make this story not very long. He hit my cheek first time when we are having a small argument in the kitchen, something very stupid. I think could be how to clean the pan, where goes the old oil. He cried after about so sorry he was, and swear not ever again would happen. I forgive him, after all his begging and million promises offering anything beautiful, maybe dress from Paris for me, roses each morning, all I want.

Maybe was a few months after, he knock me down to the floor. I was lying there and lying there, thinking now I must go. But I didn't, because I couldn't.

Just find out from the bathroom test I am pregnant, and I thought maybe we will get married. I will tell him and we will marry, and the life will be so new and perfect on the farm. He could be a good father, so quickly laughing and giving and singing our songs with me and the kids, I am thinking. I am hoping.

And I cannot help it, I recognize this baby is my safety, because he wouldn't ever hit me if I carry our baby. I suppose I am half crazy already in a trap I am making.

But stupid me, he doesn't care or cannot stop. One night I am sick in the kitchen, having tea because I don't feel well. I drop a pot, and he comes out from the bedroom shouting he has to work in the morning. I don't care, I am a bitch, big mistake when he has meet me, I am ruining his life. All that and some more. "You are letting yourself go! I will get trapped with a fat wife!" And again he push me on the floor, and he has kick me twice.

Second kick was the bad kick. I know I will bleed, and it starts pretty soon coming down my leg. I run to the mother's house, calling help across the spooking yard, and she drive me to the hospital, also angry I have awake her. That was terrible ride lying on the back, must be almost one hour to hospital in Missoula, of course I don't believe I will ever arrive there.

I have return home without our son, too tiny, and we can only visit, but then he comes, too. He cries all the time, the dark boy who knows his life is a mistake. At first I sing just melodies because I don't know words of lullabies, not any. I wish to love that boy. I give him the name of my dead grandfather I love, Mirek. And we give him everything to make it right. I hold him when I want to put him down, and I try, I want to feel like mother should. I say his name, like incantation for love, I say *Mirek. Mirek*, I pray to feel that.

And funny it is, Larry never hit me again. But was too late. Even Mirek has become a stronger boy, he doesn't have his mother's love. Grandma is better for him, and Cousin Mandy want to rob a baby she couldn't get. After some months, he is their boy who will eat more and doesn't cry so much, nickname Mike. They want *Mike* to have his room over there. Could be I said nothing. They steal him, like food from my dish Mandy reach over once and take while still I have the fork in my hand. And I say nothing.

Larry stay there till morning sometimes, and not too often I also go, then…I don't know how, then we mostly stay alone at our place working in the evenings. Fill up all the hours when we never talk, and we go to sleep at dark. We sleep apart in one room, and then we must have two rooms. We look a little bit, under covers, but cannot find love. Time passes, that's crazy, as you know.

I even think, better I go, even I fail again. But suddenly Mirek goes first, leaving from school, when he is only seven, first chance to run away, almost. Teacher says he never speak in the class. Everywhere is a shadow, but isn't the boy. For two days we know nothing, but a man has finally catch him walking on the highway, and the police gives us a call.

This happens all the time, and he goes wherever he can go. Each time is more difficult to find him and Mirek goes a longer way, on a bus or taking a ride. He has learn to travel, maybe from his mother, the only lesson, and he has learn to tell stories to people so they want to help him escape. He never will explain to us, and maybe he only runs without ability to understand.

We can't keep him. Nothing is here for him. Finally when he is almost ten, we never find Mirek.

Perhaps we don't make a good job anymore, so tired we are becoming. We hear nothing, and the kind people of the world are silent, believing what emergency he describe to them, one town along to the next one, until maybe Chicago, and then how will you track your small son? We put in some report, and we wait. In Virginia there is big file for Mirek at the National Center for Missing Exploited Kids—no, I think must be Missing *and* Exploited Children—but no activity in the file. Terrible because maybe even best news isn't going to be good, because we understand he would like any home but our lonely place, maybe we cannot even call home.

And is like he never has been there. He never stand with his long arms by the door looking back with my eyes, his chin like his father so sharp against a strong neck. He was not handsome boy, but you never know, he could become more when he is a man.

So I follow the calendar for one year, watching slowly all the weeks, and then I tell Larry we have to say everything is over. No more good water under the bridge. It won't change this damage if I am staying. He says, "All right." Nothing more, but later he says thank you, and we touch our hands on the table.

Bella, I must say to her, oh, Bella, do not stay. This is dance of death in your spirit, but worse can happen, will happen, maybe to other people, too, and you can't take it back and never goes away.

Maybe her guy—so stupid he is, but perhaps could improve—will not try to stop her freedom, because mercy is going both ways, and this is what Larry and I discover that open us a new life.

Will be some time before Mirek become like a ghost to terrify me, and his father in the shadow, memory echo.

But here is coming Bella, who has put makeup, and now looks so beautiful and smiling. Beauty will make everybody happy, even one who cried just before she pick up the eye pencil.

In Iceland, you know, isn't stripping allowed. Even is prohibit topless waitperson. This law is regard profit from nudity or some sex behavior like a lap dance, which is criminal, not because religion but for feminist reason. Those who pay are criminals, so Icelandic sex industry will die, because no money. Only country which outlaws this for equality, by the government which is balance of gender. That prime minister is lesbian, which never is going to happen around most of the world. Do you think America can get a courage for that now, after Obama?

You ask about when I strip for the first time, and what I have thought about it in those days, now ten or so years, last century. After I return from a farm lifetime, nothing is going to surprise me, not even back in New York. I feel more comfortable to be in great American city now, like another generation has pass. I have definite case of accelerate ancestry, already like a child of child of myself. I am living my life in bunch of short pieces. Seem so long since I was wife of Theodore or even mother to Mirek, and I feel young in my new life.

I stand naked, never fear myself or any person.

I always like my drinking, you know that. I am usually thinking why not I should study to work in a bar. I have still New York accounts, pretty big ones, I didn't outdraw much over years in Montana, but I want to make a life again, maybe this time down in the South. And I have a friend, or so I had believe, in Atlanta. She was talking about a piano bar when we met her, so I have the idea to pass by there and find out if she, name is Barbara Blank, still is singing, and so if I could sing there also, during bar school. Of course is now about twelve years after we knew her. Will she be singing around in Atlanta in her funny deep style? She was three or four years ahead—is she passing forty, I wonder? Can be a grandmother, by chance? No, her lifetimes I'm sure are making my ones seem to be infinity, such a mad woman if she has a vodka tonic. She would leave the bar in the morning if Theodore step up, only because she hears him, only him.

Now if I had Theodore, I don't have to go search for Barbara. She brings a few bad memories, so maybe we only sing together. And I don't have to think, what will I explain about him if she is still asking? Sometimes I think I can tell you here what mistake I did with Theodore, but unless you know more I don't believe you ever will come back. And I hate myself still and then I know I cannot be loved. Please keep on listening, my someday friend, even if I ask you to do what I don't do.

Oh, where is Leo when the light doesn't work? Something broken always here, last night the ice cubes are water cubes, and we must pretend the drink is cold! Must be connection switches, or fuses, something turn off?

Please don't give up, wait please for me while I look. Ah, where is locksmith girl? Yes, we have Annette who part time is a locksmith, beginning a trade. I asked about her father one time, and she said he is a locksmith. I told her maybe would be nice for him, if she continue his business. I suppose she is talking to him, and Father wants her to practice with him, become apprentice locksmith. She already fixes anything around this club anyway, a light, a door, a stereo, cash register, or freezer. But now she is part time here only, so this, of course, will mean parts are broken some of the time.

And when she dances, she can be thinking about old refrigerator. Not so hot now on the stage is Annette!

Do you think I know where I am going when I take that money from the woman in the Mercedes? No, I didn't see, but I could feel, just little something is wrong. But I am afraid to follow that question of why I have that little feeling, because we are on a beautiful trip to Mérida, and I want to be a fool in love. But I have just in my stomach, *something*. And when the ride is over, I remember what a funny story that was, and a wonderful day, what I told you.

We will not be fools if we don't fear to know, but we like to be fools, perhaps. Now, yes, but not later. When that lesson can't be used again, just stays hanging around in your life.

So maybe we write a song to try to understand that mistake logic, or to put it somewhere away, so isn't always what you tell a guy in a bar. If it weighs so much for you, still the song is playing everywhere you walk in the day, even quiet in the morning in your bed before the dawn is coming up.

You better make that such a really great song or you don't dance, and you know we have to dance. A tree sometimes might have to create a wind, so it can move the branches and send over a motion for other trees.

My body is a dreamhouse. Old dreams, living so long there, now they are antique dreams. I have a dream again about Mirek, always I am trying to reach for him. Sometimes my hands cannot move, and I can just watch. He lies there, on the back, infant with wavy hands, and I have no possibility to understand him, what he needs. He does not cry, but I feel some sorrow coming from him and it is coming to me. When I wake up, I am closer to memory of him, who he is or maybe was, and I feel like some love *almost* happened.

Almost, this feeling, almost. That is one of the antique dream ideas.

––––––––

Here is poor Leo in his morning beard, yes, even so late. Oh, don't say even a hello, good afternoon! He will pass by and leave his cloudy train in the sky, which I have try to change but isn't any way. This is what I have said lately to him, to explain a better way.

"Are you going to frown on me and smile to a stranger? You take some time to be polite for the car waxer, you even give him some fold-up dollars, but for me in the morning? The one you like to say you could fall in love with, like this time for *really* real? A dark frown without words."

"But you know me, so I can be who I am. This is liberty, the best of home life!" says Leo.

"Oh, for sure is a great lover benefit, this frown," I reply. "And I am so glad you give away to a stranger, who doesn't care any less, your beautiful smile for nothing."

"You want only my best? Not all of my true soul, sometimes dark?" he asks.

"It's going to be hard question to answer, baby, when you don't save any light part this afternoon for me, after I do a lot, especially smile on you."

This I learned from Theodore. On his blackest day, he would break a mood to pay a special kindness still to the people he loved, number-one people not to lose. He will tell a guy at the door perhaps to go to hell, but there can be time for a very gentle pat on my head. Or he will fold my hair, as a sweater to put in a drawer, which was funny sweet thing. Leo has to learn again how lovers do this comedy, when they need to make a bridge over a cold river below.

Theodore is absolute genius for loving. In Mexico, you remember, we must be uncle and niece, so our system is in the eyes, the chin, the shoulders, sometimes lips. If we sit in a group, it is possible to communicate by touching our own face, to wipe or brush away some breadcrumb from a lip or some hair on a breast pocket, something normal, only natural. We look very quickly, like family and always relaxing. But, you know, quite hot between us. And if I touch his arm, I am concern about his health, so if anyone notice a warm contact, he will think, oh, could be Uncle Herman's cancer, of course Katarina look after.

Sometimes I start believing he is sick. I forget we are acting, and my heart will ache over his poor walking or quiet voice. But if my eyes are fill up with tears, I say how I am very happy my uncle will live to see my marriage to Daniel.

And I pretend Daniel is Theodore when I hold his hand or kiss him. I am keeping straight, I hope!

Or I completely believe I am Katarina, with so different life story, all details coming from another childhood school and village, and of course a personality of a sweetheart bride, because lucky nobody must know really about any bride, only she is pretty and good. And the bride can be any moment at the salon or the dressmaker or somewhere she is busy, and if she is there, she is smiling and on a run, cannot stay. And this bride doesn't speak a very good Spanish, or even many words poor English. And the groom is going with his old school friends on a fishing trip, of course nobody is around most of the last days for talking.

So everything is okay, until three days before. You know, in Mexico often can be two weddings, one for the beautiful celebration, perhaps at biggest church, and the other is civil one. Love is nothing without the law, down in Mexico, you know. Civil wedding must go first, to present certificate to any priest. We have about twenty documents, but when we are last checking we discover one is not translate into Spanish, the birth certificate that Miguel has prepared from Japan, where Katarina's imaginary parents have been living when she was born. Her father was important friend to Japan, Miguel says, because is special talent for him to draw this pretty old birth certificate in Japanese characters. That is made quite beautiful, and maybe Miguel is losing the way in that artistic work and he has forget it, but we need also this translation, and three days perhaps is not enough time to prepare.

Unless Miguel can do a fast job. But we cannot find him, and Daniel says oh god, I believe he is taking a short trip on romantic business but hasn't mention destination. No cell phones, of course, which now are saving our neck—and we lose the nerves all at once.

We make a big mistake. Daniel goes to find a regular translator. He believes is only formality and any service will do it for little extra money. But this professional, how nice he is when first we go to his office, has spot a few problems in documentation. He has never seen this kind birth certificate, he says, and Daniel says, yes, is from a small town in Japan. Local workmanship, you know, a little different. Maybe he will have to take it to a colleague, he says, because he would like to make sure is legitimate. Could be like that for foreigners, you never know, or a poor copy, says Daniel, and he invent a story about terrible trouble to get it, waiting already months, etcetera.

Please, says Daniel, this is so important to finish, my love you can see on the line. My family will not live, because you don't understand how important is this wedding for all the family. Poor uncle of Katarina hasn't time.

Now Theodore is looking like crazy for Miguel, going to his home and calling one place Daniel says he has many times before taken a friend in the beautiful coast. See if he is there in Puerto Angel in beach cabina together with her, but no luck. We didn't expect he would go that far, but we are getting crazy. Because could be we have to pretend a big fight and call off the wedding, even if we find Miguel. This translator, is he going to take that birth certificate, and maybe another strange paper, to the judge? Will the judge take it to the police?

We thought would be easy, very easy. Maybe we are completely okay, so don't worry, we say. Why is this guy going to worry about this certificate? Didn't he worked for Miguel, or maybe he knows something of this artist of the museum?

Finally, Miguel returns, and he is pretty mad we haven't wait. He says he doesn't know this guy we hired, I think Bozo he is calling him, and might be he would cause a catastrophe about it. All of our fun is gone, and now we are idiot bunch of criminals, I am thinking. I was only young, but why are these elder guys, Theodore and Miguel, so stupid?

I find Daniel in the dark garden, putting around the standing *candelas*, and we talk over if we shall cancel somehow. I don't think he is afraid of his parents, but I recognize he is afraid to associate with crime, perhaps which would change his future. Suddenly I experience some romance in the night air, and I think, we must marry! I tell him how beautiful will be our Corsica honeymoon, because I believe we have to go on, and if we will stop pretending, if we don't dance on top of the muddy ground, we certainly sink down.

So we go back to Miguel, and suggest in the morning he can work with this translator and try to finish, if needed more cash can be given, for both. Yes, Miguel will take it, as credential, you know, of his *bad man* experience.

You know I talk too much when I am drinking my wine, and we stay here very late to talk. Only Leo doing few jobs kindly so I have a rest. I have stop asking myself why you listen, but maybe it is for you, because you have a great need also to be known. Every life is a song, and if you like my song, maybe your one is similar the way it goes. We have passion for the rain, for sad ballad, but also for the fast dry streets after.

Same proportion, perhaps of wet and dry, sweet and bitter. And might be a dream or important wish you have, also, of taking a secret from someone and drinking that down like beautiful poison.

Or maybe someone has sent you here to know me, so you can pull me back to somewhere from the past. Can the past exist? Maybe so if someone will not drop it, somebody who is very strong can keep it up still flying.

But I don't want to have suspicion. So funny, I am sure you are thinking, how I love to trust, even I don't believe anything can be trusted.

I shouldn't be trusted, which I have told you as I beg you to believe me. Won't you say you believe me, even when you say you do not know who I am?

No, I don't give a last name. I don't tell it. I am Ludmila only, sometimes I am called Worthy. You will know more why, and I hope you will agree I don't have need for other names.

I always was too young. Still I am, but I am older kind of young. Ignorant and young are different, the meaning can be the same sometimes but usually, don't we, it can be possible to forgive a young person for ignorance. After many years, we expect some learning. But there are persons who take that learning and accept only a few parts how they want them. That will leave them stupid, but a little like a person younger. But this undergrown character nobody wants to forgive, only perhaps a stranger.

Something changes in our wedding game. One day remaining. We continue, with some preoccupation. We have some confidence, maybe enough. Who can be sure if Daniel's mother regard the same way at me? If she didn't check about Uncle Herman during the lunch, has she lost concern or is she becoming more busy? Was someone telling her anything? She keep on asking for my health, I don't know why, and I say no, I am fine, but my uncle. He is hanging on a single hair.

I go to his room, and we have a chance to make love. Gift of the gods, Theodore translate to Greek, you know. This is happiest moment of the wedding, because we have to be so quiet, and we are never quiet, and make sure three times the door is locked. Theodore at once has a strong back, not like Uncle Herman bending over just little while ago with shaking cup of tea, and all his skin has blood, much more red blood.

After, we look out the window and notice it is so windy, and we are hoping for calm coming over the celebration. If Miguel just complete the last document and we see the judge later in the day for Part One Wedding Ceremony, the drama and the music will commence in gardens below, tomorrow at four o'clock. It is all ready to blow away like a memory.

"See you in Corsica, my dear love," is whispering Theodore as I go out.

Poor Uncle Herman, I will say to the father, outside just on the stairs. Very worn out he now is.

Did I call Barbara Blank my friend? Maybe you have very many people you call this, but I am not sure. I will not ask because I believe this question we mostly don't understand how to reply, so actually our answer will reflect only hope or despair.

I know just that. Barbara Blank will not sleep on the floor for me. Anyway this capability we cannot find often. Camus—oh, he is our author of one of Four Books, did I say?—in his novel *The Fall* has told a story about a friend who will not have comfort in a bed so long that his friend suffer in prison. In his own warm room, he has made himself that promise to sleep on the floor, because only he could do that much. Theodore often has mention this, when we have been speaking of Daniel or Miguel or Mrs. Finch, if any would have offer a commitment in solidarity. Finally, there was always only Mrs. Finch, but perhaps we will never know and only because she is dead. Only the dead are standing by, or lying by, I suppose. On the floor or the grave, wherever they go to be our best friends.

I had some trouble to find Barbara, but I won't bore you to explain, only say in those days, it wasn't search by Google. Yes, there was probably Google, but I didn't know to use that even few years ago. I went person to person, by postcard or a telephone or on the street, until there is Barbara at the wide-open door and looks like she didn't change. She didn't go to distant planet trying to find love and make a family, and lost a lonesome boy and her man, maybe, because she doesn't look out from a mask, I notice. She has her beautiful face still, and it smiles all the way. By that evening we are having our drinks in her new club, in Backwoods, I think it is called, and I am introducing to her friends and really we are not friends, I and Barbara, but we have our understanding from those old times.

Thin memory, now you can see through it. Maybe friends, we would have to tolerate them and could never get rid of, anyway, as Clamence has said in *The Fall*, so we can be satisfied if we have understanding. And lucky I am, Barbara will have a bed for me, and she has her own one, even there would be someone suffering still in a prison.

No bed will be comfortable, but I can sleep most of the time. When I don't sleep, I imagine I am someone else, one of those characters from days of Theodore, maybe a guru follower or better a banker, and then I sleep from boredom.

I take some time to hang there, Barbara's old visitor friend, and one night I play few games of pool with guys. Just eight ball, and I scratch on a first shot, and make a lot of nonsense excuse and throw my temper on the second shot, because I miss it. I put bad wobble in the stick when I hold it quite far over from my body, and I shoot over a flat hand. This is what is expected. But really is no fun without

Theodore, who taught me the way how to be a fox, and now I can use two hands and put in contact lens, so there is no trouble to win. But I save some tricks for hard times maybe coming up.

Theodore like to quote always from Camus's book, about every intelligent man really want to be a gangster and rule by force over society. It must be true. I believe this dream is a very strong one for some men, like Miguel and Theodore, even while they maintain a good profession. Because isn't dangerous to grade student assignments, you know, isn't heroic on a horseback or taking all you want, asking no one. The power of a man has no locked doors, in those dreams. A man must have more names, also, so he will double up to be two men. More women, too. That is reason for itself, don't you think, because an intelligent gangster has high chance of sex.

Better than we can see, for example, in the life of Morris in his university office. This poor example can drive out of there a man like Theodore very fast. And he cannot tolerate to go back to his lecture, where now the student even can have more power than has a lonely professor, dusting all those old books (but doesn't remember his jacket shoulders).

I don't like to carry a secret for someone, even my own secret will be too heavy. But I have to carry a little longer about Theodore. You will forgive me, because I am leading to truth when I don't tell you, even lies are going there, I always remember from the Four Books. Now let us have another drink and watch a show.

Comes out soon our favorite dancer. You laugh when I always say that, whoever is coming on the stage, but don't you know it can be true that moment? Why not?

Daniel comes just after to my room, and says, yes, something is wrong from his mother. Somebody has question her about Katarina, and because that she is asking questions. We have Miguel just finished the translation, all the flowers are here, and his mother asking questions. He told her nothing, but promise we will come to her before dinner. Now the group—oh I remember the fear taking my body over with burning!—has to meet to decide, and I have the plan. I was thinking as Katarina, so I know what can be the problem.

She must be a Jew, I say. Because Daniel has told me the parents don't want that, and try to conceal they are anti-Semite.

Once he had a school friend, which they didn't support. They always find a reason not to trust him, but he was very kind boy. And probably, Daniel says, himself he often has wondered if could be ancient Sephardic Jewish part in the family from Spain. Aguilar, you know, is name from his mother. That is the worst for anti-Semite peoples, because anger about it is quite deep under and often nasty fear is crawling around not to be found out.

So now I think if Katarina will tell her childhood in Czechoslovakia, with immigrant Jewish father and mother from Germany, poor life after the war, discriminate from all sides, they will forget legal paperwork, or who knows what suspicion they have. Those parents of Katarina are not allowed to speak German in public, and government won't support that language in school for Katarina, and other Germans have been run from their village, and maybe killed, even though the war is over and they are Jews before Germans. This story I have from a woman could be ten years older than Katarina should be, but this Mexican family will not know.

We haven't time, and they haven't time. And that is helping us. The mother first is very angry that we lie to them, and cries about how sad and ruined is the whole wedding, of course for her, but Daniel says, but no, we never want to conceal. In fact, he will tell everyone tomorrow on the wedding day about his beautiful Jewish bride.

I can't ever forget her mouth, when his mother says *won't be necessary.*

Look like she would spit her tongue, if only possible. She is tasting shame, I believe. And you know, shame is quite sour together with hate. I don't have hope to change such person as she is, but how good is showing their disgrace when they cannot avoid to see it, too.

On the next day, we are married twice. First in the morning, in the chamber of Justice, and later in the church. Oh god, I mostly hate every ceremony, which after you don't easily remember anything except the photos, but really it was a beautiful one, best of all how Daniel looks so handsome when we are dancing! He is proud for himself to abandon his family cage now already behind, and he has developed to a strong man, really you can see fast transformation. And we feel good, like skiing down a sparkle mountain or surfing a high wave top to the shore. It is last day of our job, and even tired our backs are straight.

The honeymoon tour goes in the morning, and even though with a hangover, we are so glad to take a plane out of that place we know we will never go back again. We arrange only to drop all the checks to Daniel's bank, because when we all arrive in Corsica, we need to be very rich.

New plan coming out of Theodore's folding theater is going to be a big success only if people there want to invest in what we are appearing. If we look like we have something to take, they will come to us. And only then we will help them discover a way they can give.

So at first, we require a shopping trip, which who can complain. In Porto-Vecchio, we go to our lucky hotel, you won't believe. Hotel le Roi Théodore is there, beautiful with four stars, we could never resist to stay there. And we arrange to pay for superior room for me and Theodore, under Daniel's family name, of course, Madame et Monsieur Zaragoza de Aguilar. Daniel will take a separate room, so lonely after his marriage, too bad. But soon, you know, he will find a lover, probably could take two days.

He has old friend—yes, sea cottage was too solitary so we change the plan—and they will meet. Maybe he will stay to play more games with us, and he offer to make a friend to people at the yacht club. Daniel most probably meet there some film stars who will take him to other beach around, and discover perhaps a party for us all.

Such a blue water in Corsica keep us so happy for several days. When finally Miguel came to have a week, with money from some of our gifts he has been selling in Cancún, we had even more celebration. We got more money, much more for each, we couldn't even imagine. Daniel wrote a letter to his mother and dad, to say we are safe but will extend very long honeymoon across the world, and you might not hear, even a postcard.

You ask about Tiffany, how she is doing in Vermont. Once I am glad she called up on the phone, and she has wonderful news and definitely landed and will call soon, but nothing more, and I couldn't absolutely understand her, and she hasn't left her number or any address. So I feel disappointment she keeps out of touch all this time until now. I wish so much to hear about where she is, in her study of cheese in one of those Vermont farms. Leaves are up there now turning all fire colors, but blue, maybe not. I imagine that country place when smokers come in from outside and still puffs it around, like a cold air you see it, or when you walk just finding there a horse in the way. My fantasy! Instead Chevrolet dealer on our road.

Bella didn't show around here today. I hope isn't trouble at home with her guy.

Some days, you know, there is funk. Leo says that, *funk*, you can't move it. I don't get out worry from my head all day about my friends, these women who are not afraid enough. If they will be hurt, might be I am the only one who cares, and I don't understand how they didn't get better love. All the time it shows up, do they catch it almost, or love is coming out like perfume from a bottle but doesn't last?

I wish it would be fatal to be often an asshole. Maybe it is really. This guy who beat up Bella maybe is not going to die immediately, but down the way could be we don't know the cause of death is not cancer. Autopsy doesn't show any information, but life stops from pile up years behaving like incredible asshole. Do you think we know everything about the body?

Somebody report on the news yesterday about death really could cause by a broken heart. Sadness shock completely can break the heart, now they see, just muscle was fine and suddenly becomes weak until fatal. After love stories of all those centuries, now we believe because of science. It's Official Broken Heart Syndrome, of course.

Acting terrible and violent will last a long time, I am sure, not only for any person you are hurting, but for you. What pity. If you don't want to end your life so early, why don't you stop kicking or hitting a small woman? Or make her feel stupid and weak most of the days, and when one day she is strong you better fuck her up? What pity if you don't control to be an asshole and then you die.

I don't know if Barbara is going to rescue me or I will rescue her. Probably it is both a little, because we suggest for the other ideas, and sometimes even same one. She provide some dresses for me, because I have been on the ranch, and I don't know any style for these days in the city. She has offer me a chance to sing a favorite song in her bar, and the dress we select is blue midnight, almost black, lucky about my size.

I hope the patrons will not ask me to take it off because they didn't like it, but I never think I have to take it off because they like it very much. Barbara has not prepare me what these guys are expecting, but she suggest I go to a lingerie store just for new foundation, maybe with lace and some wire under, to fit that dress closer so I feel I could sing better! We are laughing about feeling sexy, but I don't notice really what idea she has. Is her club, and she will make a right costume, of course I imagine.

I suppose I insist to be innocent, because why not? I never think I will join those dancers in the back part of her club. No, because I want to be a singer and torch dancer, not a sex club dancer. But anyway I can be anything, I discover that on my way with Theodore. Nothing will touch me, if I always keep the good and protect my passion.

Maybe you don't agree, and in some case, you are right. If you kill someone and still think you are good, you are crazy.

That night I don't take off the clothes. Is only test run, Barbara says, to see if I could have a success on that stage. The music is not so good, because I haven't practiced enough all the songs. I wanted most perfect to be the ballad by Cole Porter, "Everytime We Say Goodbye," but I wasn't very. And I have really disappoint for myself and for Barbara, but I notice the patrons were not so sorry. And they clap like crazy, so we sit for a talk the next day.

"They like you, Lude," she says. "They like you to talk and they like the way you move around. You don't need to sing. You need to be burlesque artist."

"I thought this was history," I reply.

"No, I think you can help a revival in Atlanta. We will work on costume, and watch some film I have," she says.

"Dancing with fans and feathers, like a drama, all that will be popular today?" I ask.

"Something different. More funny and sexy than is exotic dancing," says Barbara.

So we have try all that, and guess what. Is popular, because even naked dancers can be boring if you see that all the time. Even most beautiful body needs a mystery, a fortunate lie which is provoking a fantastic surprise. Good challenge, and I am going to play that part very well, which Barbara knows. She knows me and Theodore when we are working at top of the game.

For a while, why not imposter stripper? Could I be an actor someday, with opportunity now for practice of art on the stage?

One more life I change into, very easy just for now.

But I don't know if I can live imposter life again. I have been a mother, I am a mother. I say it to understand how that happened like takeover of my body by space alien, without proof so even I may believe it.

Perhaps I am imposter mother but I never change back.

I am thinking dinosaurs again. This afternoon I don't feel optimistic about the world. We are close to front of mammal line, oh yes, humanity's self-extinction could happen, not just you or me going alone this time. We cannot live chewing only insects, so when food is run out and shortage of grain and rice and meat arrive for poor peoples, we are sinking, not just from oceans rising up. We are sinking under wars and terrorist attack, not only in Iraq or Jerusalem or New York, but here in Tampa or even Brandon or Lutz or Largo, the small places next, and constant, because fear is everywhere. Your friend or own brother is desperate and he steals pure water from you, because costs more than he has, and he must drink and his wife must drink, and tomorrow, too.

Seawater will come in from Gulf, and contaminate water will come up out of the sewer, and your dog will float away.

Yes, it's true, I didn't sleep last night. Leo keeps me awake, because he doesn't sleep. Sorry for my stupid talk that doesn't save human race, only make you want your drink faster and hope your favorite dancer will soon appear. A snack if I can find any in the back, if Leo has remember to take out frozen breadstick from Italy we are going to try.

He will sell the club, he says. And I try, at three o'clock in the night, to talk him out, because he cannot go on the road, someone like him. He is not like Theodore, able to make a new way each day, and I think he imagine it will be possible for us to go like that anywhere around the world.

We are going to see. Today maybe he will not call real estate company to look around here. I hope he will have faith, yes, in our new ideas for this club, because we start to make progress in our business, and Leo's family property will be worth a lot more if he will stay some more years. But he is missing his music business, and we don't have yet all the possibility to create again here what he has lost in California. Perhaps his own music studio one day on this spot, who can say?

And where am I? Where are you, after you have no more need for love stories or dancing women? Or any excuses, even for you yourself or me? We find our way till then, and I hope we don't stop sooner.

We have to hire a new dancer now—someone testing out tonight, I hope she will be so wonderful as we think. Very pretty black woman, and we decide her stage name can be Carmen. When I told her what we pay before tips, she is quite glad, and also she cannot work more than ten hours in a week, and I said isn't a problem and you could later add if you want, there is no top limit. She heard from Bella is a good place to work, and Bella told me hire her right away, absolutely.

Some pretty women are loners, because they could scare men and even other women, jealous ones or just anybody who fear the power in strong beauty. If possible, we bring some friends together here, and try everything not to make competition. Even in this small club, we like to have three dancers always here, so they are working together but not opposite. In the perfect world, all should give a hug and forgive totally in case of disagreement. If we have laughing here, everything can be okay.

Now back in Corsica, a little danger on a cruise boat for our friends, could be time for karma or thinking twice.

Invitation on a yacht? Who will say no? Especially not I, because I have dream of the sea, early on in my life wishing some opportunity will open up to become a sailor. I contemplate and contemplate on how it will be to float over the deep darkness, and I want to sleep over it during nights and work in the day as on land, whatever I can do.

Philippe Corréard—name is famous, perhaps you know—he is our host on the boat with his girlfriend from Germany, Ehrengard. I remember quite well how Daniel is mad over Ehrengard, and so I worry before we go, and I make him give me a promise about nothing going on. No extra trouble, please.

But everyone feels high-degree confident, even probably myself happy not to be careful, and we don't see it.

Too much wine and too much vodka, too early in the day, too far out at sea. Everything is fantastic, and we begin to discover about each other, until Daniel lost a little patience and cause our host insult over his manhood. It is for Ehrengard, but doesn't seem so clear, and Philippe goes below deck. So not to push Daniel over to the sharks, he says.

After we rest, I put on a new silk dress, and Theodore his new clothes, too, and we go back up on the deck to start again. Mix a drink, have a party for sunset. But Philippe has turn the boat, and we are at the shore! We don't get second chance, because Philippe is a quick man, taking off from trouble on his instinct.

We learn. We understand time will soon come for break off from Daniel, because we cannot take his word. We must be like Philippe, fast and final, but how hard after I have married Daniel, even false marriage. I will confess part I love him, already like husband, and now what about divorce? Perhaps we say, for anyone back in Mexico, we are not happy or have a big fight. Or should we talk about option we never consummate? Can we throw out the marriage?

I think must be better to have at same time only one husband. Maybe life could be quite convenient, without extra husband.

We have to take our time to separate, because Daniel is going in a sensitive transition, says Theodore, and we know he would like some adventures with us for a while more. But has to be done, before we take another risk. No more danger in a boat in the sea, but let us first have a beautiful holiday for the four!

Theodore then will speak to him about his future, with Miguel, fathers for his new life. They want him to do better, hope he will be a good man. But during this holiday, no lectures for a young person, oh no. Daniel is a free man, and far to go. Who is so lucky ever, just married and looking for lovers?

Harmonic Daniel. I watch his love affairs at the beach with Françoise and Dominique and so on. I wonder who teach them, all those French girls, how to move. To be beautiful is like riding a horse or driving a racecar, so magnificent how delicate is every move. Partly we see, but partly don't see how they make it. Natural is almost never natural with humans, and least with feminine ones. I think this art is fabulous.

Sometimes the car crashes or someone could fall off the horse, and then, my god. Often we agree when ladies didn't reach it, and they try most of the time harder and harder and fail. But how can achievement of real beauty be bad? No, beauty is always good for any person who sees it, and doesn't matter for what it is when it comes. Beauty has no obligation. No law. It is for everyone and no one.

We eat from the sea under stars in Corsica, and everyone would like to be in love. Only Miguel is old loner without luck this time, but still he seem to be satisfied. We are all friends from a sport life which isn't simple to play, so we admire the other and we remember about proud people when they fall, even we haven't push them.

Serious moment finally when Miguel has to go back to Mexico City, and those guys sit down for good talk with Daniel. They don't say we cut him out, or I want to divorce. Only, stay for a while or go to another place for this summer, Daniel, but find your reasons well. Don't always float. And be good, be very good to your life.

And we exchange address for one definite place always we could find out about the other. I tell him I don't know if we are going to be safe, and he should be safe. We give him our love, we take Miguel to the airport, and we board a boat to Nice, why not, on the South of France. Theodore has a great wish to visit a gambling house from a book he read. And we must stay in the Hotel Negresco, very famous at French Riviera.

On the boat, Theodore and I look back to our work for Daniel, and we talk and talk about if we did some good to set free our friend. That family we met, it was power and nothing else counting for them. They keep him in a pretty prison of greed and prejudice. It is true we went in there and took more stuff, when we took Daniel, but we can't calculate the balance. We just never can know it.

We wonder what is any effect for us, something is possible to notice? Love is better now, because we have joined in ancient ceremony of breaking, but it was law, not bread. But you can say bread we shared, I think, also.

I prefer not to lie, but Theodore likes difficult puzzle for the mind and likes also to hide safely the truth. This is a kind of person Camus talk about, and reading that book Theodore understand himself. He was used to say truth blinds and lies are beautiful twilight, something like this from *The Fall*.

I have told you Theodore look to be changing, and I am from inside not able to see him quite clear. Maybe in twilight, I can't see he is mutant or anyway could become a stranger, man who could shock. When you are together with someone for a long time, you carry first days' pictures and stories with you. You see those, too, when you look at your lover, now after years and years. When you die, the survivor lover cannot live anymore without the better parts hanging on.

You don't think we are better when we are younger? Not more innocent? Oh, innocence is not goodness, you believe, and you are right. But innocence is sweet, even remembering could make you better, not like a dried old cake. Like ice cream on the top, you should take it.

I don't call you sweetie, so you will not call me honey, all right? So funny this is, don't you think, all the time putting warm cover over cold, a nice word at end of maybe a not quite nice demand? It won't help, not really.

I want you to understand I am a good person, you please know this by now, and I have more to go. I won't try to cheat and call you sweetie.

My mother was used to say about somebody, sometimes me, *meant the best, did the worst.* She knew my nature, my curse. I don't try to say I never have known what might happen, or I always was innocent. In these days on the Riviera, I was growing up. Middle twenties, not yet end twenties, but going on the wiser side.

Why I haven't left, or even try to fight against that direction we were going? Remember I am like a girl compared with elder guy, also professor. What will I know? Have I experience of literature or life or love? I believe Theodore has found out something about the world so important, maybe not happy news but true, and could be his search is the best we have for great life together. I remember those days I have my questions, but no answers, so I try to stop asking.

And then I stop, enjoy a ride. And I don't start again until the bad thing happens that I will later tell you.

For now, yes, a martini cocktail! With olive, only one so not to fill up, and dry like a desert, and cold as possible just before top will be ice. Thank you, my friend coming from where, I don't know.

Snow is never going to fall here in Tampa. I got after a while used to that, and probably vodka even is better when it doesn't snow. But sometimes after two or three martinis, I imagine how beautiful would be a palm tree white with snow. And then once in little while, I am having stupid nostalgia about home. Or sometimes I remember Montana one of the beautiful days, and it happens suddenly to make me cry.

Living in too many places, you have just the spiderweb roots spreading out. Anything—could be breezes!—will pull it out and you topple over. Here the sand will not take you back. You blow off down the road again, singing your new song.

Oh, you wonder about my stripping, you devil! Okay, we return to Atlanta to see what is going on up there in a crazy club more worse than here.

Barbara knows this burlesque act starting back up from visit to New York club, I think was Slipper Club or Supper Club. She has ideas about new burlesque, should be for modern women and men, little bit ironic or feminist, you can say, and fun. So we go to thrift store for costume ideas, and we get big bag of crazy ones. We find cone bra with stitches from 1590 or 1950, and old red satin nightgown, funny silver stiletto shoes, a giant Chinese fan, one small blue parasol, and a very wide hat with feathers standing. And old corsets, short or long and white or black cotton. And then I put everything on and take it off hundred ways for her, drinking glass of wine, and we laugh all night. This will be fantastic, she says, and then we fix up tall hairdos and put makeup to try everything to make a character who is ridiculous, beautiful, and totally sexy.

First night is great success, even I have my high heel broken from those shoes. I make it a joke, and start a jumping dance. Maybe doesn't sound funny. Leo says often, *You have to be there.* I make a story that I wait for my husband in the bedroom, and practice for him. Kind of old-fashioned drama. Character is not professional, so striptease has some failure and quite funny, I believe, sometimes a piece falling completely down and she put her ear on the door then and begin again a new idea.

Each week we offer two shows, and every show is another concept, so I am at the store always or testing out for Barbara what idea I imagine, could be a dream. I love this. One drama is in the garden and I am cutting flowers and bushes, but every time my clothes— I have bought fabric catching on or grabbing on—it will be thorn sticking on, and comes off completely. Finally in the private garden I will not bother, and continue without any clothes, clipping on the fence until suddenly I can see some audience over top!

Some very innocent and kind of silly, but other ones are more wild or more normal striptease. Always more patrons coming. Barbara is so glad I turn up there. We are like sisters for this time.

One night late, after she had been singing a great show and we are talking at her room, I tell her about Larry and Mirek. She hears everything, very quiet. She won't judge, I am sure.

"I wasn't going to say anything," she says then.

"What do you mean?" I reply.

"So funny you mention, because someone came here for you last week. You were home, and they drive up to the club. I saw a dark boy in the car, teenager age, I think," she said.

"Who was it? A man? Was it—"

"He wouldn't tell his name, but I know he must be from when you were gone."

"It was Larry, must be. But what did he want? Did you tell something about me? Oh god."

"No, I said only we are friends from many years, but he knows that. He said he is going south for vacation, but he will come back this way next week or so."

I must have told him and even don't remember, about Barbara Blank in Atlanta. It was trouble for me to find her, and probably was trouble for him too. But what they are coming here for? How did Larry find Mirek and why do they travel on family vacation, like regular family, down this way by car, such long way from Montana?

It has been almost one year ago I left there. Two years since Mirek was more than a ghost.

At first, I want to run.

I see how you look at me. How a mother could feel that? But longer I am away, more I understand I was dead, and everything there that happened was to a dead person.

Oh, I want to smile. I want to exist again in a past with Theodore in love, in France, in life of music and money pouring all out. No person knows who you are and nobody will care to find you, only strangers attract to you and look into your eye, fascinate by you.

We do anything, any day. Perhaps shop for a coat if it is cold or begin to rain, and our coat is back at the hotel. We get sick of the antique coat, completely mad for fresh one and yes, latest Italian boots. But soon, we recognize we have to stop or must do another job.

And you guess it, we can't let go a money lifestyle. We hang at the bar in the best hotels, you know how grand are those old fantastic bars, and we offer a drink to anyone nearby to us, to start conversations. There is music, beautiful people, laughing elder men with young women—people like us, yes.

Always it helps I like to flirt. Eye contact across the room when Theodore goes to the bathroom. I scope everywhere for a handsome man first, often he is too confident, or a man having some obvious weakness, maybe is short in his legs or has comical ears he attempt to cover with long side hair. Or he has new jacket, very important won't fall off the chair back. Some indicator of self-conscious circumstance, and always his eye on the move all over the room, to see anyone has notice him.

I am that person, with kind eye for him.

I appreciate him in his strongest moment and the weak he can show me, too.

Later when he has pick up my scarf when I walk to the bathroom, his eye is quite warm, and passing by again, I invite him to have a drink, if he likes, after his coffee. Definitely he comes. Sometimes Theodore can be my uncle again, other times he is friend or company colleague, but never could be my husband. Always he is very friendly to the man, too, and we are so glad to make acquaintance.

Theodore remark many times, maybe it was one of the Four Books, that hardest thing is not to take, when you don't really want. It's too easy, and becomes habit. We like to play together and win, always win, and after we should stop, we keep playing. Like gamblers.

Maybe once you had gambled and start to panic. And some excitement partly it was there, and you want to beat it but also keep that going on. You feel sick and you feel hungry—what is this? New kind of happiness.

Reflexive. Bad behavior is quickly turning to reflex. You don't have to think, and you don't want to think. We are like skaters dancing together or like high wire walkers finding a next step. We rescue the other every step.

And we rescue the man—usually a man but few times a woman—short-term rescue, because later we have to drop him.

Let us consider you have come over for that little drink. You want to find a way to get something from me, probably sex, or for the least, some attention or favor, maybe another invitation, a chance to have a connection, I don't know. But usually, there is more than free drink that you want. And I will by the end add your guilt, so you don't later track after me. And you never turn me in, because you are shamed by yourself.

I tell you my uncle is not well, after he goes away to bed. We have a good chat by this time, all three, and Theodore already has practice a wonderful charming but very sick old man.

"Shouldn't he transfer in a rest home?" you ask. Or maybe you will say nursing home.

"Maybe so," I answer. "Maybe I am selfish, but I don't want to put him there, and also I am alone, don't have anyone else. It's so terrible, and I think pneumonia now is back."

"But you must get him to hospital, of course!" you reply.

"But this is the last trip and can't be shortened. He would die."

"In the morning, why don't you let me help? I will be happy to drive you. You must not risk his life for a holiday only." I see you want to be good, and show me how good.

"Oh, you don't understand!" And I begin to cry, and always I feel actually the pain of losing my love, and I go on to cry more. You take my arm and pull me over close, maybe your hand is sliding on my breast for a moment and then your chest on it, and you hug me very hard. I keep crying, you keep rubbing me.

"We have no money," I finally say. "He is just broke, broken man…" I am softly sobbing.

"You don't worry," you say. "Here, let me buy you one more fresh drink."

"Oh, no," I cry, "I usually don't drink, only tonight, I am so worried. Oh, all right, little vodka, so I sleep. But you will have one, too?" I see you are definitely drunk, and a strong desire to make sure about tomorrow is growing. You expect I will come to you if you start to open your pocket. Already you imagine my body smooth, my fat breast in your hand, pumping going on below. You hear my soft voice calling your favorite words.

"Here," you say. "Take a few hundred for hospital cost. And there is more when you need it."

"No, my uncle will be angry for that. You don't know how proud he is."

"I have lots of money, only tell him I want to help," you answer.

"No, you are so kind, but I'd better go now to bed. And I can check on him, take a look if he is okay."

"Please," you insist. "Let us only finish the drink, and maybe I can persuade you to take my help, after you hear my own story."

You see how it goes, and this is the bread and butter, nothing to do it, and in the morning we are gone. With his hangover, our man will look around the hotel next day, and feel his sorrow mostly about not going in my pants, and only little anger for himself not to make it. Later, when he is buying a newspaper or croissant, he will see how hundreds are gone, but never would call the police because he was begging me to take that for two hours, well perhaps one hour, to accept his offer to sleep with him. Which I never take, only finally the dollars. I agree only to sleep on those, and I say probably I will give back at breakfast time.

If he thinks more, he may see his own darkness where he is looking for mine. And he could see himself wanting that. Happy sucker, Theodore calls this kind. He loves to give away his real world, what he consider cheap.

This was training. Transition from our job in Mexico. We had to practice much more for future folding-theater productions.

I tell myself it is drama. I don't allow to think it is, yes, robbery.

Those dreams start in Atlanta, like ones I had about paralysis. In Montana, if I didn't dream it, I woke up like statue, flat over, and spend all the day in bed. Or sometimes all night and day couldn't move, and even didn't get up to wash or to eat. Must have been depression, but that time I didn't know. I only understand the world has nothing for me and I have nowhere to go. I can't even wish to die, because that means to want.

I want to move in my dreams, though. I want to run but can't.

When that car comes back to the club, I contemplate to hide in some part of city away from Backwoods, or Buckwoods, where I am living at Barbara's place. But I am totally nervous, really screwed up. My stomach must be full with acid. I have to go to New York.

I told Barbara to tell them now she doesn't hear from me. I am with my new boyfriend, must be moved away. She could pretend being angry I didn't paid her.

"You are sure?" Barbara asks.

"No, I am not sure," I say.

"Stay, in that case, because you bring it back if not," she says. She knows what is to regret, and I notice over her shoulders going a shiver. But I suddenly think of that tall ranch house of brick like prison and long dirt road away too cold to walk, and I haven't learn to drive a car, and I hate even to remember those years.

"No," I answer, "I know where they come from. And where they return. If I am one day ready, I have that address."

Before I go already I feel sorry. But who cares? Who really cares? Because you know what? That car never drives back up.

Here around Tampa sometimes Leo and I have been on a horseback ride. We love animals and sight of hay and dirt, even if we don't have skill for riding. Down Brandon Way, past all the supermarkets and dollar discounts and Kentucky Chicken drive-ups, there is pastures and quiet country. And we will drive out there, sometimes just for nothing drive on Sunday morning. Traffic goes the other way to church, and we have our church out there with the pigs. Also wild turkeys and deer, you don't expect in Florida how much wildlife is there. We keep their company.

Smells of nature can be a message of meaning. If you have only false aroma, some fragrance in a can, you will have nothing to comprehend. Even in a smell we consider to stink, there contain some idea to contemplate. Yes, it may be danger, don't eat this rotten fish, or it is there for saying, you are too far from your humanity, remember that you also can smell, as any living body, and will definitely smell when you become corpse.

Darkness coming over us here this afternoon, my friend. But you knew we were going deep, so no surprise we must have a party this afternoon. Yes, right away! Let us bring out some chip and dips, some beer to put in the champagne glasses, white chocolate from Switzerland, and music from good old banjo days or why not calypso? We will take Leo out from his back office where he lives too much, or too little! Maybe Rebecca is in the bathroom cleaning, I think so, and she can join.

If you can't go to the country and smell the shit until Sunday, have your party in a dark room. Pretend it is midnight. In some case, immediately almost could be too late.

If we survive to tell more, you and me, maybe we board another boat, a great big ship that will like a star travel across North Atlantic, or sail away to Trinidad or even down to Rio, or just stay in a casino for a lucky night, you know we always hope.

Do you know Claudine Longet? What a sweet singer she is! I love that song in very funny movie *The Party*, which I have seen many times. Henry Mancini wrote it, called "Nothing to Lose." I can try singing that. *Nothing to lose, if we are wise, we're not expecting rainbow-colored skies, not right away, nothing to lose, it might be fun, no talk of spending lifetimes in the sun, although we may…*

If Claudine Longet is still alive, I don't know. She did kill her lover, everybody knows was homicide, after his cheating. And got away, only negligent penalty. Yes, I believe this is true.

It is so easy to betray your lover, isn't it? I admit I wanted to often go with Daniel, too, but I didn't. I think about him still, because his love was strong for me and raises me up to those rainbow-colored skies.

No, I didn't hear from him since four or five years, but I saw Daniel again, and he had grown back straight, and he was going to be a man who stays far from trouble like mine. Still he had not married again, and we laughed about his *one true love*. Was he serious? I won't know, because mostly we can't ever know how we have importance. Some years later, a guy tells you you are beautiful, and he thought always you were, or he wants to see if you are maybe now alone and will date him. Shock to hear it, you don't know what to say.

But I'm pretty sure I knew then Daniel's heart. In different circumstance, our marriage in Mexico City might have been a real thing.

What bothers you today? Did you woke up with memories of old lovers? Are you sorry you let someone go, never follow up? Did you have to tell somebody to go away, not call again? Your body weighs more on the days you carry around that sorrow, hasn't it? Your legs are slow lifting and your back bends farther, like Andy coming in here on his walker, ten or so minutes from his car in front! Ancient one didn't come this week, and I wonder. Maybe one day his desire run out for beautiful dancers, you never know.

Your face is folding up.

Take your mind from that, and look over those hills with cows we paint on these walls of the bar. I will take you over the hills. You don't have to travel away, you keep your identity here, where we look after you because we know you, one of us who wait for a while to get somewhere else.

You don't have to speak. Only let me speak, one who need to put words like paint on a wall, over and over perhaps the same wall. Our time is coming when we finish and the painting will be worth to look at, maybe not beautiful, but worthy.

I wake up young again today. I stretch out my body and turn like a fish, and I laugh to feel so strong. What happens? Do I really know if the truth is inside or outside myself? Does it hide in a mirror? I think I get power in the night, sometimes, like a charge up for cell phone. I work on a problem in sleep, and I wake up decided on how to go.

Let's talk about our first trip by ship, the *Stefan Batory*, in 1987. Theodore always hear for years about a chance to go back to New York, first to Canada, on freighter boat, which is from Poland but goes over from London to Montreal. I think was about a week or two we took that voyage. There we were on the beautiful deck chair with blankets, reading possibly the first time one of the Four Books, or in the Grand Lounge hearing Strauss violin concerto, dressing in a best jacket, and for me a black skirt I have to the floor. Or in the dining room, having sausage and potato dinner, and for dessert my favorite profiteroles or chocolate cake—wonderful menu, classic everything as from Poland. Real artists performing for passengers beautiful music all times of day, for teatime until late dancing.

Crossing over North Atlantic, we need music because, oh god, this cold journey and the storm we never forgot, three or four days rocking over and up and back down and back up, until we couldn't eat or take a bath or nothing else, just stay in bed sick. When we feel better, we try to make love but are too weak. I wonder if Theodore will be too old for me, sometimes he cannot do it. But I find in New York was only the seasickness that keep him down.

We wish, even so, we had years later chance to go back home to New York on the *Stefan Batory*, but hasn't been at sea anymore for very long time, since the next year after we went. Now we have roll around down on the Riviera until we are sick of games and need ourselves to rest. I want to go to hairdresser's shop to fix a big mistake on the back, and Theodore has to visit his doctor after two years, so we decide to return home, to normal. We contact a friend of Miguel to help us to make again my papers, and then we can go. We have to declare less money than how much we brought, but actually we leave with same amount of dollars.

"We weren't here, I guess," says Theodore. "It was another couple having so much adventure in great hotels? Maybe we only dreamed."

I recognize I wish it was. Only a dream, not the life I am living with Theodore. Yes, it was adventure, but where is our real place together for man and wife? Can we hold our head up? Whether we go to New York or we go to Madagascar, we have to know more what we are doing. Anyway, someday.

So I get very happy when Theodore has call New York to his university to check what is happening, and he discover there an offer. They need a lecture for someone who last minute can't make it. This guy he knows for many years, but is emeritus or senior something professor and, too bad, isn't longer around now at university.

But best news was that lecture is touring on board a cruise ship, and too lucky for us, it is not that far to catch back to New York, and Theodore will have his chance to talk as professor again, maybe about the Four Books. And I know that will make him happy, and bring our life back to ground. Or I suppose not to ground, but to water!

Have you hear about great literature for cruisers? They offer now instead of hairy chest contest for traveler who doesn't drink cocktails all day but would like to cruise around the world. Lovers of education also can have a good time, you know. If you can only give a break or two from swimming or gambling, they will like that.

After we talk to this professor, John, already he was preparing for boarding in England, and we learn he has had appendix attack, serious one. Theodore agree we will come on board in Cherbourg, where *QE2* will take a last stop after crossing English Channel, to pick up few passengers before straight crossing to New York. Six fabulous days and no charge for our voyage, even for me, says John, and he will try to clear everything with booking office in I think Miami. We just will get there in three days and climb on.

And John advise Theodore to speak only about Melville, because he is seagoing writer and will be perfect for cruisers. *Moby-Dick*, says Theodore, no problem. We find immediately English copy, not too old one, and he is smiling when I look at him open that right away on the street. I think, this is good to fix his heart, to have break from Four Books ideas.

We are so happy when John can call and fax and make it go for us, and we have those days to travel north from South of France and prepare for sailing. I have imagine a long time to go again on a ship, and of course luxury trip will be more fantastic. I like this real woman I will become once more, even I am still called Katarina for a while. Yes, we have to take this character back to America, where it is true, Ludmila never left.

You come more often, don't you? Now you look less on the stage, and sometimes you eat a sandwich while you watch a dance, or you come over on the side here during dancing, even before a break, and you ask me to continue. Sometimes you have to tell me what was yesterday. I like that help to keep going on track.

Maybe you like me to hurry—no?—but I can't let it too fast out. It comes in pieces and together only at last, as you carry off what has been my life.

We have made a quiet music policy for between dancing, you know, so constant banging doesn't give Leo headaches. Or me. And we can listen and talk more here in the club, and it is more social opportunity for all the guys and dancers, too. But also isn't required and nobody bothers. And we make it nice, don't you think? I think we have a bar cat soon, if I will bring inside one who would sit on a lap—ha, no, not a lap dancer cat! Leo, always serious manager, says what about any allergy of patrons? We still must talk it over.

We do not sell a lap dance here, no, even is popular in Tampa. We don't have to do that. When patrons are touching a dancer, you have too many problems hard to manage. Best to just say no, isn't offered here, you know, and keep control. If someone is not satisfied, he may enjoy bar down the way, and we can wave him goodbye. Poor Buddy, old timer around here, has to transfer, he told Leo. All right, says Leo. Not too much a shame, we all agree.

How much of yourself are you going to put on a sale? If you will not put your naked ass into a stranger's lap, is possible to stay a distance apart from handing yourself for cheap sale. You sell your image, yes, perhaps a story of who you would be—but not all the way to the bones.

Leo doesn't want that kind of whorehouse business, and like anyone will do, he decide where to draw a line. He anyway can be condemned for profit on the body of women, but for himself he can stand there. Nobody coming here get a chance to know him, really. Most nights he goes in the studio, he make it soundproof, whenever a chance to write his music or something, I don't really know. We are together apart, some new way for me. It's okay, we have respect. I know, strong word.

Looks like we are going nowhere, but we both always in process, some shifting or resistance going on. So much like you, I am sure. Parts inside are trying to move like plates of the earth.

I am just back from hospital with Jolie, because the tests came not clear for her little son Nicholas. Yes, you remember the stomach?

Maybe disease of the intestine, so they are doing now a colon test. Poor boy, only eight years old, and looks less. He never grows because he hates to eat that medical diet. Jolie is going crazy over that, because she reads about autoimmunity or chronic problems that hasn't cure yet, and her doctor would offer a smile more often, she believes, if there is hope.

What can I do? Only go to be with her, she said.

I look at Nicholas and see a boy who only would like to play on a stupid computer or even, yes, go to school. You cannot make him laugh now. If I try he will look out of old eyes at me, staring like he doesn't comprehend what is a joke or he cannot hear from where he is, only beside me.

Purpose of our story is to try to save each other, so beautiful, but we have no possibility to succeed, at last. Along the way, yes, we grab a leg out of the lake or we lucky put on the brake, but later we need more saving, and more. Could be we love it because then we have prove what is impossible, because in that moment we explain a miracle, what never can be.

Did you ever see a body giving away his flesh, starting to go? If you lose somebody slowly, you watch his loved flesh go pound by each pound, until he shows you the bones he would like to leave for you. Oh god, I don't want to see this small body leave his mother only that.

Yes, you knew Barbara Blank has betray me, and this I told you before. She would not sleep on the floor for me, but worse. Leo writes a song for me about her, "The Ballad of Barbara Blank." These years later, I told him and he wrote a blues ballad, so sad and kind of blessing to me. Later he will sing it for us here, and you will learn that story. I shiver first time I hear him sing it. I know Leo has been understanding me, forgiving me.

But today please, if you won't mind, let us go on board *QE2* to see what Theodore and my old self—or young self!—are now doing. You wonder?

Drinking. And much too much for both. Rum with nothing or with anything. Some days for lunch and steady on, with sick headache in the night, and hangover till lunch. And steady on again, if not we will be hating ourselves all around a clock.

Is not sudden, we see. Too much time in the bar for month or two, in France, before. We get frightening. My heart is fluttering at night like birds in a ribcage. Promises, promises, every day broken but not forgotten. It is crisis, we know it.

Queen Elizabeth is a party, best one you have ever had for six days. No one can say no at any possibility. Luxury is on your hands like extra time. Theodore give his lecture and is a big smash for us, everybody coming by to meet expert on Melville's great book. Fascinating, they all say, and now they are going to read it, finally. Sure.

Even so we are beginning to fall. We often don't know about last night, and we can't remember three days before. Theodore got sick one night, very sick over toilet, and maybe I am blacking out one or two times, if this is when even someone explain everything ridiculous you have done, you don't recognize any detail. Theodore looks old, having much more creases, with red skin patches and kind of blue nose. He is pushing on fifty, should take care. When was he last a kid?

Talking in our room before we approach to land in New York, both we decide to knock out any cocktails for some weeks, maybe more. We hate to. Maybe go in the upstate country, and every day take long walk around to watch for birds, climb on trails. Theodore can wear his many pocket pants, and I have some boots for that, hikers.

We meet very many people we like to see again on that boat, our dinner mates from Italy, those two crackpots, and casino friends Big Laurie and Scott from Chicago, and really we hope they don't remember drunks, only drunks, when they have a memory from us. Who is the woman, can't catch her name, who told us we are in love more than anyone she ever saw, true lovers?

We fall in love again, I suppose we can, when we stop the scam and come home in our own shoes together.

More I can do, more I can do, I always think about this place. Not only the walls or the snack menu or the base pay of dancers. I want the place of work to meet needs of workers, first before patrons. We want to be best club, high distinction and profit, of course, but more. More today, not next year. More if you want to take a week for sitting at hospital. More if even your mother would come over here for a nice drink.

Well, okay, she must have unlimited mind and sense of humor, but yes, she could come by. How nice would be to meet Jolie's mother if she can visit after the surgery and take her mind off.

Nicholas has operation tomorrow for colostomy, and we hope not permanent. Can be sewed up again, if his condition will be, maybe not cured, improved just. So sad for a young boy, my god. What can we do here at the club? Flowers are not for a boy. A game will break his heart, because you don't want to play if terrible pain.

I must take an old cat who likes to stay on the bed, once he is little better. Then we can bring the cat over here, or give to him to keep, if he loves her. I will ask Leo if we can go to Humane Society, look for old girl left behind by her family, maybe they lost a job and couldn't care for her, and she has only few days before the limit she can have that cage. Hospitals allow sometimes this kind of visitor at recovery, and maybe for such a sick boy, if she is very healthy, and we will check everything.

A good cat will keep any pastors away from his room, keep out church ladies wandering with boring ideas for children. Nicholas must have reason to live, not hope for death from too much praying. Did you meet ever so lovely boy, so much joy showing before he has become suddenly sick?

Crohn's disease, they mention now. No cure, only management. One of rare, very early case, doctor says. Misfortune, terrible. If we hear him laugh again, this will be beautiful. Can we save him for a while, so we have his pony laughter long enough to record in our minds? How long is that for his mother or grandmother, or for me, or you, who meet him only playing a card game of Fish in the quiet afternoon?

Jolie has confide on me, parts of her life she doesn't tell anyone. Once she wished Nicholas had not been born, when he was coming and when he got there, in the months after.

"I stopped having choice," she said. "I couldn't see beyond obligation every second for rest of my life. I even must watch out when he goes to the bathroom, every time for years. I knew he was beautiful, but I wished I never saw his beauty. I loved him, but I hated him because he never goes away even for one hour.

"I would always have to love him. He cried too much, and I never thought I could make him happy." She was post-partum depressed, as probably I was. But for her, the baby wakes her up and love comes so strong, soon enough to save her. And child and mother come together, work and play and grow. She will make him a fine man, she believes, and her love for him never she could imagine to be without.

And now, she will live without him, but never the love. And Mirek walks the earth, without luck to live with mother's love and no chance to give it. Each day I don't find him, I rob from him that, a human right for relations.

But can be forced, love? Could I make you love anyone? And without love, could I make you give your lifetime?

Now some days you want to argue. You ask about why I don't let Leo offer here lap dance. If he will do it, we could have more cash in the club. You ask about my child, as if so important, more than me. And still every day we let children die, or we kill them. Or we sacrifice poor mother for any kid, maybe a lousy one.

What I have to stand up for? For who? Who is a judge?

I have torment but isn't because anyone would think he knows I am bad. Or maybe so, maybe you know.

Each day any small danger, one mistake under more and more, is in our next moment. If you will make one step you are so brave.

Do you know a person who will not laugh? I know so many. And I sit to wonder what is happening that somebody wouldn't like to laugh. Do you think they haven't a laugh to give? Or isn't ready to hand over, like fold-up dollar for the porter? So they miss that chance.

Or is a laugh too much to give away? How much will it cost? Is it shame if it goes in someone's ear and you let him get your feeling?

But for what emergency condition you need laughter? I hope it can save for best time later, but I don't think so. Cannot find it to-morrow. And yesterday you were sorry only, not laughing.

Suddenly feelings will appear, so wake up! Isn't forever to catch it.

Long time ago sailing on *Stefan Batory*, they have Midnight Sympathy. Is quiet for all hours when anyone could be asleep or only peaceful resting in the dark. Or perhaps making love. Or thinking. We show sympathy if we make this silence even for thinking. And we don't knock on the door or crack on the floor. I often remember this system of the ship from 10 p.m. to 7 a.m., and I consider like a law, when we need to have more understanding about fragileness. Nine of twenty-four hours, definitely isn't enough sympathy.

Here at our club we don't have sympathy at midnight, not that kind.

But I wake up in the night sometimes, don't you? I am like a sweater unweaving. Like a book all pages scatter out in some few piles.

Other stories I have, you know. I don't know what to do about all my stories. One could be more important, but I forget about it. Or I want to tell and decide not, and later consider I should, but you are gone. After ten, I like to have you here, so you will understand me more, but you are here these days in the early day. You go sometimes before dancers come even. Only you stay when I talk.

Now you call me Worthy, very sweet.

If I am busy, you even go, I notice. You don't get your drink if you will sit alone, so I start to wonder if you change something in your life. Maybe you are expecting something.

If you are listening for the answer, it will come.

My beautiful dress could be the answer today, don't you think? I love it, how can a dress do that! Soft and silk, yes. And you notice this sleeve is slender, couldn't fit everybody, so was a sale dress. Thank you, I like it also very much, so maybe I wear it tomorrow again. I hope I still will like it tomorrow. Sometimes is already gone, this feeling. A small problem I didn't see now suddenly there, maybe doesn't fit to one shoulder, or design isn't so right for me, I consider. Could be only my heart is low on the next day, and I become not so pretty and nothing will look nice.

If it will be cloudy, this dress stays in the closet, my heart on different sleeve.

The bar, why I love the bar? This bar is only like home. Isn't it some kind? Not public, not exactly, more private place for people. I think you can become like a family of strangers in this place. I like more here than Leo's big house to sleep. Upstairs is warm where I sleep many nights, sometimes with Leo if he would like to be with me or doesn't want to drive so late over there.

We have transit relationship but staying, isn't going anywhere. We stay in this moment, like a Buddhist love affair.

I resist to future plan. I forget to remember.

Many things I don't anymore remember.

I think I don't lie, but if I don't remember, could be I have done it. Can you say is correct all your stories? I can't say this, therefore I confess to be a liar. Mrs. Finch told also some lies, if so, but I think only incorrect memory. She didn't know it.

I can't feel sure. Sometimes I have suspicion, yes, I hear what I say and I don't believe that is right. But I don't want to go back, because I can't fix what I said, never. Next time trying won't be better.

Probably crazy, but I will tell another story about love. Not a Buddhist love. You know I fall a lot in love, so still are stories in the old sack from days before Leo. Yes, could be Atlanta one or even New York one. I make it true story, don't worry, so true as I can. I think is stupid to say, but if I don't say that, you expect some lying, don't you?

Funny if a person says, *I have to tell the truth now*, or he says, *To be completely honest*, because you expect he will lie then! You listen more close to see if he shows he is lying, because you absolutely know he is lying. This is old truth, but still people often like to say that. They want to promise, to offer guarantee. Ha!

Every woman have Married Man Story, seems to be. I don't say guys are, you know, always going to try out something even if married. No, but could be pretty common.

I know how his passion is growing while he looks another direction, take his mind back but cannot. Suddenly world is moving, and worse is in the car or train because that will increase. He feels freely going away, or forward, to the lover.

I know, you laugh about my analysis. I do it always.

Bar philosopher extraordinaire!

Don't laugh, isn't funny this phenomenon. Velocity and infidelity corresponding. Also cold weather, especially snow. Factors could be very ordinary or original mystery, first time you imagine that. Normal could be old tragic love film. Not so normal might be oatmeal breakfast or what, circus advertisement! Anything going on mostly will happen to provoke it, because romance is like soup, can contain spice or cream and all between to make more. And forbidden soup has all variety to become very hot.

My case was very sad for children. This is often fact that doesn't matter until late, and then if it will be possible to take that back, he will give his life. Or he would say that, when he most feels that pain. Maybe on a birthday, on a phone call from far away and he can hear the party, and he must make it short for her. It will be too short, every call has to be for both, and now he recognize it.

But he didn't come to me when he leaves the wife. The wife only has to learn about him. Then she prohibit everything and his normal life cannot continue. Broken down, all that.

So easy! One look, and follows one touch, and there is earthquake beginning deep below in the mountain, and many people are going to lose home.

Javier has his own smile, nobody has a smile but him, you think. He must invent first one. Even all the guys you know, still could be a surprise for you, like you have wish upon a star. Nothing like a drama, just happens and you don't feel shock from that, only you know it very strong.

If a man is a brother of your friend, or friend of friend, you trust if his misfortune story is sounding to be true. But so many men can be brothers, and a man is not more honest having a sister. Anybody will know this, but who is thinking all the way?

If so, you will not care if somebody like Javier is, okay, very nice. You will not start to wonder his strong back or his neck, what will feel like in your hand. How is beating your heart or shaking your hands, or if out from your throat shouting will surprise you, soon when you go together. Might sound ugly but couldn't for you, and not for Javier.

Even one time, you won't believe, Mrs. Finch had married lover. Yes, and she told me about a man from downstairs, I think a doctor, and then she said, "He was my lover." Didn't say more, only filled up her eyes and look away. But finally she laughs, because she likes to talk about love, same as I do. Do you think it is terrible? Who can stay quiet? Maybe the same person who is keeping laughter in a happy bank.

Is love pure? No, and I don't wish, because humans, you know, never going to be angels. But I hate the children suffering, even all history will tell this fact of life.

So we have Javier. Or I have Javier.

New York guy, city guy, broker guy. No, he didn't go to Barbara Blank's place—I knew him late before we went there. My friend from a dressmaker shop, where we keep arriving at the same moment, strangers, a few minutes only. One or two times looking at his eyes that are stopping on me, and we know already too much. And then I make a real mistake, and I haven't draw over that curtain enough while I try out my dress.

I see his eye seeing. Blue lace, too late.

Sex isn't started but already can't be halted. We are ten feet away and too close. We talk to dressmaker in code of double entendre, for planning, darkest planning.

"If it will feel too tight," says Javier, "I like it, to begin, but later I have to take it off before I can relax."

"Oh, I like it big for me," I say, "but in some places little smaller."

"I'll pick up on Friday about 5:20, but if I have to wait for few minutes or so, is no problem, I don't have evening plans," he says.

"Is this dress finished by Friday? If possible, please will you call me? You have home number, but here is a cell phone, because in case I am riding subway, even last minute from downtown," I say. I hope he has good memory and when I give the number, I repeat.

His body so near, how to describe? Good danger, standing on the edge but safe enough you can breathe, and you can see far below strange beautiful places.

I don't know he is married. But I don't know he is not married. There is no time to have my hundred answers about who he could be. I have one answer for my question, what if he never stands next to me after right now?

This won't begin Buddhist love affair, you can believe me that. Anyway not at first. We start out typical desire for some sex.

Oh, but you don't laugh. This must be bad story for you, too. Are you child in this, always going to be child if you hear such story? This is Leo, too, son of cheater. One morning he hear through the wall his mother talking to her lover, by telephone, and he cannot understand how she talks because he is young and never heard that. She doesn't talk that way to him and not to his daddy, but maybe to the puppy, but no, isn't short word or two. More like song, sometimes like crying but most times like happiness. Then he hears every day this love music from his mother's room after Daddy goes early to his work. He doesn't know Mama, he realize, and he became afraid, and didn't want to eat his breakfast anymore.

What you are asking? *My* breakfast? Yes, I did, and lunch, too. Of course I eat, I am not air plant. My own tomatoes, peppers, broccoli all growing in the back, in buckets on far side of the parking lot. I don't like what they sell at Publix supermarket, because no taste in vegetables and who knows what country they are growing stuff. I eat mostly without cooking, often I am having salad only at lunch, and in the morning cold cereal. Leo pick up a baguette some evening and we eat like a picnic, you know, fruit and cheese and wine. But without blanket on the grass, just here in cement building, with breeze from air conditioner.

Maybe I bore you? My old story of bad-behaving love? You know why I tell you is because something there you must need to know if you will understand rest of bigger story, right? You have to pick up that along a way.

Here, I make it better. Have a taste of cheese from Tiffany. She send us this kind today—strong cheddar, very good for bones, she wrote. Yes, now we hear she is okay, and she learns to follow that profession, because we believe in her.

And in the package was include a photo of her friends there. And her lover, I think, beside, because I know how Tiffany will smile, so different, if she is in love. We never see that here, all those teeth, even in the back. I don't think she has put even a lipstick, and she is more beautiful. A builder woman, so tall in her working boots.

I would give her the job back if she will one day turn up here, like a daughter return home, but I hope I never see that.

Or maybe I don't. Maybe I will lie, even if we need a dancer.

Theodore was terrible one night, such a bad liar in his folding theater, that I cannot hold my tongue back. You think we are lovers and never fight, but we have that history, too. We have been trying not to drink, and nerves are short, you know. Our mind is always saying, why not one drink? What is one drink? Then our mind is laughing about how stupid our mind is, and we know better. What sad conversation goes back and back again some more times in silence between us! Perfect hole to fill up with fighting, so we have no way to stop it.

I comment he is bad con artist, really bad one. Better be careful, foolish little professor running after excitement! I am laughing, but there comes awful sharp voice I notice. He looks over to recognize, to believe I change to that sudden witch—we are at a car show in New York suburb, I don't know where—and he calls me worse.

"Little tiny nobody from nowhere, *you* are," he says. "What do you know?"

I remember that, all the words. I walk away, because I can't be near him, but he follows, speaking very softly behind my back.

"How would you know if I am smart if you are not smart?"

"How smart is to live," I ask, "in a bunch of old books? Do you understand people here and over there?" I point around, which he will hate. Always he want to appear so cool, watching other people but nobody watching him. "Maybe they know more than you, ordinary people just selling a car."

"You would like that, if I were salesman," he says, "because you don't appreciate any wisdom, because you have no education. You don't know even what you should know, you have no shame for not knowing."

I am sure he doesn't love me. He never did, I think, and he is right, I am a big fool for following him away from my home, and all these years, oh my god, what will I do tonight? Nowhere to go, because my trap is closed very tight. Any move and I hurt myself, more than him. I can only cry, which seem not to have a point.

"I have shame," I say.

"Yes, good, you should have a lot, and get more."

Life is really shit in America with this old guy, I realize that. And worst he is right, I am stupid, every reason he describe and also one more, to be so stuck in the full shit here. I could be happy, I am sure, anywhere else, near or far.

Maybe was sign of trouble, but next day we are kissing up, and afternoon comes and we like to sit in our new Buick. Well, not new but perfect for us to drive down to Atlanta, where Theodore and I last were together.

Bubble of marriage about to pop. What is left over after a bubble? Some spot of soap and dust of memory, only that much to dry out and disappear.

Mrs. Finch went to church, looking around there for some forgiveness. Or she said, "To stop the pain if possible." This was when the lover told her his kid was destroying herself. Probably, who knows, she spies them in the building or she hears her mother cry. This daughter has cut her arms to bleed it out, and scars will always remain, so Mrs. Finch goes to church to see if she can stop thinking. All she is asking would be that or maybe to stop loving her married man, because if she keeps loving she cannot stop it.

I wish to find a place, I don't care if is a church. Imagine this switch goes off and you don't feel your regret! You could try a drug or take a drink, but you know it will become worse only. Angry and sick for something you do to take pain away, this will fail. You go ahead searching.

Mrs. Finch couldn't find God.

She found a church, and religion is there, that was very quick. But no god for her, not sitting inside the door. You can say she looks for something too simple, and it's very big, and she can't see that it will take a long time to understand. Mrs. Finch didn't want to change her whole life—no, she believes there is just one part broken.

So next idea is a tool for this problem. Keep looking how to fix with a small tool, she says, even smaller and smaller is the way, maybe, for a heart breakdown. Maybe one word or two, maybe a song, maybe a garden which is growing in child's hands.

Or a bird goes over there with his everyday song. Talking, talking about his business, funny bird knows he is important. Somebody, perhaps a little girl, has seed for him and will wash his cage.

Mrs. Finch buys a bird for a girl, and her father goes with his cage back home.

I don't know what is the ending, but Mrs. Finch always suggest a budgie or a cockatiel—no, not a cocktail!—for any kids in trouble.

Her story. Typical style, doesn't go back to the lover, doesn't explain. And you have no wish to ask.

Over there is Leo, we will now wave. He has been trying to *watch*. I told him this is his problem. He is not a watcher, and if he want to make good strip business and help us run our place here, he has to learn what everybody likes now to do. Be all the time viewer, see constant video, look at behind action scene. Try to peep, I recommend, or come in here to sit and look at the guys who look, and see why they always look. Try to know what interest there can be for a customer.

He of course likes women but can be bored about looking at not much going on, but boring is okay, he told me, so his imagination will be able to occupy his mind.

Now there he is, but like a boy in school, just waiting for a bell. I am cracked up when I see him, because look how he isn't watching, only thinking about anything else, not Carmen how she is dancing most of all for him. Today he said the world will come to the end, and everyone will be just watching, each alone, probably.

I like him. Funny man, hard to turn on by the stage but a good lover for one woman. Lucky for me.

But you know, can't probably teach constant watching or even understand that, if you like more to *do* something. So I don't think any hope exist for Leo as a bar owner. Every bar is a place for looking, even our place must be.

Leo lives in his ear, only for melody. He even doesn't wear a nice shirt, and I put that on the chair for him, but he never remember.

You see I can watch. I like to watch him. You think I am falling in love? No, I don't look for love here.

Okay, everywhere, everywhere I do.

My mother. Again you ask. You believe I don't have love from Mother. You psychoanalyze about first memory—or, better, first mammary!

Oh, god, roots again you believe I must find. A long time ago, Gregory in Key West is driving me crazy about that. And on a photo he gives to me, he put on the back, *Find your roots from where you came*, something like that. I didn't know he took that motherless child photo, yes, a sad young girl I look.

Hangover I had, so terrible that day! Nobody has a mother's love the morning after, I told him.

But kind men are coming to the bar, acting like the long-lost mother, if you are fortunate. Thank you, maybe I should say to all, and I don't argue.

"You are young once," says Theodore. "Once only."

"I would say that you are young many times, every day for many years, so you can't count it one time only if you like to be accurate," I reply.

"You know what I mean," he says. "We're not going to have opportunities endless in front of us, enough to throw some piles away. In your middle ages you will see this," he says. Now I see he is right, but then, I don't care.

"But how stupid is to think you have to make whole bunch of fast decisions because one day soon you will be old and no way back! Who says if you are young and when you are old? I hate that," I say.

"I don't want to argue about any of that. All I want to say is perhaps I won't return to university," he says, looking direct at me. "Haven't we come little too far? How will I go back to students and explain it's very important where to put commas?"

"Don't you think so?" I ask.

"Yes, I do," he answers, "but not *their* commas. Their ones are like toenail clips, little disgusting even if put in a correct place. I am so bored to sit and look at a comma now, when I have been to Corsica with a beautiful Bohemian bigamist."

Suddenly we are laughing, but actually, often we argue now days. New York isn't good for us. We hate the subway in a heat wave. The noises of ambulance reminding of nuclear disaster all day long. The neighbor has a recipe of garlic only, garlic with garlic sauce and garlic salad. Theodore, if he sleeps, sounds like a lion angry with hiccups and that wakes me up so in the morning our black eyes are meeting and we run to start coffee.

But money. This is a question, if there will be enough to always make more. Insurance for doctors, condo, Buick, etcetera. We don't believe in money, not this usual kind, anymore. What money must do is now all coming from magic, anyway we think so. Or it comes out of crazy ideas, from novels or theory, big one if you squeeze it hard.

Theodore isn't fifty and I am even not thirty, and nothing is wrong.

Back at old university, Theodore has Morris with his sweater next door. And Marguerite with orange branches. And commas, fascinating like toenail clips.

In autumntime, they expect he will be coming back there. I don't believe he can delay another year if he would like to keep the tenure, so he must decide what worth is that in our life.

I wonder if we should return to normal professor couple. For a try out. He quits any time, why not, if that game is over. I suggest that, but he will have to think if he can tolerate, if he should for us or should not. In a long view, because he is young one time only, and like a markdown sale or an easy mark you have just to grab it.

He has some ideas, of course. He talks to Miguel about medical excuse possibility, if he will provide a good documentation for the university which force them to allow more time. Is a doctor in Mexico able to speak about Theodore's disease? What can it be?

When we bring our dilemma to Miguel, we understand our hearts. We want to go again soon where we can change any facts we don't like. And we want to play our games more and better, not for money—it's for something else we get. I still feel hungry for that.

Like sex, you have agreement to take or give. You play about who will be on the top, or you put under you the one who will submit. In the confidence game, both agree to betray somebody, yes, even if it is his self, for passion in the moment. The stranger knows he will take a risk with me, and I know I do it too, with him, and we are in confidence, in play together, wanting all. Can be a little nasty. It's so dangerous, so sexy. So good for a woman.

On the top, she is more equal. Her location will surprise the man, he can't help that, and then she has more power. Until he falls, begging or crying or never going to know he is gone, under even lower, because he feels at the top. We are dizzy, meeting each his own face and the other face, over again.

We are living, we know it.

And if you have partner, like I have Theodore, then after this you also have sex, or maybe you say *fucking his brains out*. Double advantage.

Now, please, what do you choose when Miguel offer his good news: Theodore has severe intestinal infection from Mexico and lost thirty pounds still fighting that. Himself Miguel will testify as doctor, if anyone would require he must travel to New York for classes, not advisable. Not until chance of survival is much better.

Sometimes those university kids come over here to our club. They see we have different scene going on, so word goes around. These two come in again with their girlfriend now, at first looks scared but then she is laughing about our fat cows, the cows we painted. The young women should come here more, take it back from secret night place of men. Can you imagine if we can fill up with women and we don't have a chair for the trucker? Maybe a trucker has to ask a woman to bring him, or he might be scared until he sees our cows!

I make sure we have a fine wine, not from Australia, oh please. And some song collection from women. Now on this Thursday we have Joan Night, all the Joan or Joni singers we can find, of course Joni Mitchell, Joan Armatrading, and Joan Jett. Yes, also Joan Baez. We keep on getting ideas of more Joans, I can't remember all. Leo is happy if we make our original soundtrack, and he is working in the studio to operate that. Carmen says what about advertising Joan Night, with free admission for any Joan, even if anyway we don't charge.

Okay, says Leo, we can afford that.

He is like my father in his jokes. Every man has something of him, either bad or good. But I got the fear over, one man is all.

Auntie on the farm, you remember? She told me about her brother, youngest one in the family, my father who orders me out of his house. My house.

"Your father's shame is destroying him all the years," she told me. "He thought he had been a Jew when he was a boy, and even after the war he waited to be discovered. But one day it wasn't the Nazis but the survivor of the camp who came to our house, to get back his home. And your grandfather refuse to hear, because he was living there for two or three years and by that time pretty sure that owner was dead. But he was not and came back from Auschwitz, arriving outside the door talking aloud to everyone, some he knew as he knew Grandmother. He didn't have his family—wife and son, two brothers, uncle, I don't know what—but he hopes they can find him again there. Grandmother wouldn't come out, until finally ran out after him shouting that he can go to courts about it, but they won't move."

Auntie's story gave me a shock, because I never heard that. Who knows? The truth is coming, I think. Now I am adult, learning everything about my life.

Auntie told me, after he died, that my father believed I am not his child, my face was more like a man on another block. They knew

him, my mother liked that guy. Sad for me, I could not make my
father love me, and I am so foolish trying with all my singing and
dancing, but that was not enough to forget my face.

Or maybe I only heard this story, or in a dream I have explained
it. Maybe I was hard to love kid, and it never was his fault. But Auntie said my father couldn't even wait for a good excuse to kick me
from the house.

"He always felt persecution and was looking for the antagonist,"
she said, "wasting his life with that. Even when he could find a cause,
he wouldn't find courage. We were so poor for those years after the
war, and he even had to sell every apple from the tree and after beg.

"And he often told his first memory, but I didn't remember it,"
Auntie said, "the police coming for us at the house in the Jewish
street, to transport us to concentration camp, and we had to show
our papers, and they looked at the papers as they were false. They
took our father, even very sick, but the papers had been approved at
the station, so he came back. Maybe our mother told the story over
many times, too many, and she told about later what happened, even
continue worse after the war for Jewish people.

"Mental stability can be lost that way," she explained. "You can
go on your own way. Don't carry with you what your father has carried, please. Now you know it, you can throw it away."

But this is why I never talk about history, because soon you carry
it again, whenever you even remember your questions. And Auntie
was right to tell me, "Don't carry it unless you will be okay to live
like your father."

Also, I can't completely believe that. Nothing of that is written,
maybe in a letter, anywhere, and I think my Auntie is losing her
mind in those days. Her life could contain a film she saw the week
before. The history of the whole world is taking place in the field
at her farm. Or, in fact, just a few kids are climbing up the trees of

the orchard, eating pears and apples before it is time. Getting a sick stomach from sour fruit, as normal, every year just like the last one, when we all were children playing.

I wonder if you saw a tall bird outside today—Baryshnikov, I call him. When he lift up like a dancer—a real one, you know, from the Bolshoi—I felt my tears coming, it was so beautiful. This week he has been landing here, I think, to see me, or to let me see him, I don't know which is it, but we have got a connection, this great white bird and me. Florida heron really will make your mouth drop every time you see him in a parking lot. Yes, he parks here! And I just go out the door and park also, to talk a little bit to him about what we both are doing here, waterbirds far out from water.

He wouldn't know how we dance without our feathers inside the club, and maybe he wouldn't like to see that. Or opposite, he feels shock about my stupid dress. He doesn't show any surprise to notice me, only he seem to want something.

Is it water? There is shortage of rain, and I wonder if he can find water, because we don't have some lake or river very close. Maybe there is condensation catching on every leaf, only that, and in the morning he has to lick it from there. Has he got a tongue?

I know little about how to help any friend, and nothing more or less about Baryshnikov, dancing here now, too. Our first one outside, completely nude but no violation of ordinance!

Should I put a dish of water for him? Or a fish? What kind of fish, how big? Leo says he will eat about ten fish every day, so better I don't start to feed him like a lost cat.

Leo says he can fly anywhere for his groceries.

"Remember, we have to take the car, but he flies straight over there, anywhere, and pick it up fresh, even without paying," he says. "He's only lazy and wants table service. He has spot a sucker."

Okay, okay, you want to know about Javier, I know.

Why he was important is not about sex. You want to hear about sex, I know, but this is a case which will disappoint in the sex category.

We didn't hit off, after we got to bed. Closer and closer, less and less desire, until we must do it after so much trouble, but we don't care. It was not to be very much sex for us, and it has been used up already by imagination. He has a nice body and he says I am looking good, too, and there are not any problems, everything is functioning. We finish and we immediately are talking, and our talking is much better, and we don't want to stop the conversation. I am serious, we talk about three hours and didn't know it. We are kind of new, old friends.

But you can't be friends, not like this, meeting to talk out of your heart. You can't love someone who is married, just as a deep friend. Nobody allows this—you must follow rules and have sex, if you want to fall in love with a stranger.

And we both have another one we are supposed to love to really know like that, and be known, but can't at the moment. And you guess it, I was still married, too, to Theodore, and this was not after Montana, it was before. When in New York the last summer nothing was beautiful.

It's true, I was terrible, and it was easy to be terrible.

Look around, so many people alone. Sorry, I know I change subject without explaining, but just for now. This is Mother's Day, you know. We thought to close the bar, but some people don't have kids or mothers, so we don't want to keep them at home to feel lonely. And some of the dancers are younger women without family or having nobody they love to celebrate, so they will come to work, no problem.

And I am technical mother. I carried Mirek. I sang lullaby in his tiny ear at the hospital to stop his crying, and when he comes home,

same song without words. He went to his father's people, and he
didn't want those ladies, or me. Then they didn't want his trouble.
At first, I knew—the mother idea is not for me. But still I don't feel
comfortable with and also without child. Really I don't like to think
about this holiday, and I just go to the garden. I wonder if it is a
sad day for many women, maybe some are living like widow of her
child, and what if people are celebrating around and she would like
to forget only.

But now two or three guys are coming, ready for fun. Sick of all
day the holy mom story. Here, we will have some songs and a party!
Oh, good, it's raining—how fantastic for Baryshnikov!

And do you believe that Leo and I have taken a full soap shower
in the hard rain two or three times? It comes off the roof—yes, that
water is pure as Tampa air, oh god!—and over on the side of the
building, of course after hours, nobody sees us laughing in the bath,
shampooing our hair with Herbal Essence and so forth!

You laugh at me. I talk funny, I know you think. A guy the other
day said, "You're not from around here, are you?"

I said, "Yes, I am. I'm living right here, for a fact."

He looked at me again, closing his eyes little crack. "I don't really
think so," he said.

"Are you from here?" I asked.

"No," he says, "I'm from Carolinas. I just pass this way."

"Then I was first, a settler here, and you have to believe my word.
We sound like this on this road, and we always have been here. Right,
Carmen?"

And Carmen copies very well my accent. She says, "Totally, we
are natives from Florida, you really can believe Ludmila."

When I have a mood to do that, I make up any story, as we did
years ago in the bar, Theodore and I. Like children many people
enjoy to hear a story, even if it isn't possible to be true. I like it, too,

all stories, true and false. Or dreams, if they make some sense, a little maybe. I think we can't stop telling stories, even sleeping we keep on.

I ask how everything is going, and I try to fix some past problems in my dreams. Maybe I am in my mother's kitchen and we are just having conversation. Yes, I went away and stayed a long time, but I am back now and talking about her hair or my hair, nothing important. I have brought some shoes as a gift, and I hope they will fit, and she says my dress will show the neighbor lady I can buy top designer label in America.

Everything looks normal in the old house, where I never went back.

Oh, yes, I telephoned her when I was in Corsica. I couldn't say, of course, why I was truly there. I told her I was married, but I didn't tell her twice married. I don't think she felt happy I never called up before for a couple of years or so. I had only lies for her, but I could not lie enough to say I will come to visit or soon I will write.

There are children in the kitchen dream. My mother is younger. Maybe one girl there is also me, from the past, and my brother—yes, I have one much elder brother, never was close to me—or maybe it is a new family she has, second time around family. Replacement husband and kids, because everybody left in our one. Perhaps I offer her a better family, normal style this time, when I have this dream.

A second-chance life you really can sometimes get, even if that happens only at night in your dreams! I always have a gift when I am in my mother's kitchen, shoes or some clothes for her to wear. And she feels happy with that, and we talk about nothing.

But now is a long time ago I saw her or hear about her. That is the world that seems to be the dream. You can forget it like a dream, even, so you can imagine only a broken part of that dream and cannot ever fit together all those pieces, other ones that disappear already in a distance.

I was going to travel back out west, once, to Colorado. Not Montana, so help please lord above! When you are in trouble, you don't run after more, of course.

You know, I am sure, that I have been in some trouble. Theodore and I both, yes, in Atlanta. And when I lose him—you know I have lost him—I consider perhaps I should get out of town. Get lost. Go west, where you can go free. And I thought I could find a legal help in Aspen, but I had only a stupid idea.

Theodore always had a plan ahead for us, he was working that out in his notebook, watching a calendar. Of course, he has to remember the semester coming, if he could stay sick or must get well.

I never know if it has already passed the weekend, or we are waking up at Wednesday already. But now I have to know a few more things like what the day is, and also solve a big problem fast, jump to the next rock in the river. And the rock across, after. I know I will be slipping, one of these rocks.

Why did we ever stop there, in Atlanta? It is because Theodore's friend wrote a postcard that took such long time to find us. We should throw it away, but we consider maybe is meant for us to go there if that postcard has been tracking to New York, then followed to Xalapa, and then to France, and then find us in New York again. They were Rolling Stones friends, fans of rock and roll together in seventies, and that traveler postcard had the red tongue of one of those albums, I remember. Steve said he was going to open a nightclub called Mexico City, and Theodore should give up the straight man life and manage that business with him.

I can't believe that bar's name—in Mexico City was the wedding for Daniel, of course—but Theodore told me they are also fans of Camus's book. I forgot about the bar in *The Fall* that also was called Mexico City, and those classmates were always talking about this novel in graduate school. I know Steve is a very good old best friend, from ten or fifteen years back. Theodore says, let's have a little visit, that's all. Our Buick will take us to our destiny, and he sings, *Like a rolling stone,* in voice of Bob Dylan.

But kind of funny, on the way we recognize we have been ourselves taken. We stand in the road on the side, by our new brokedown Buick. Hot in the September days still there, in Virginia, but we really laugh. Even us, we can be big fools, if we need to feel happy so much we don't take care to inspect that car before buying. When we just see this pretty, so pretty blue Buick—our favorite car must be blue—you remember we have been fighting, and Theodore want quick fix. We got quick broken!

Always a lucky side, so we find a place to have lunch while the car repair takes longer, and we talk to people there about our new club we get started in Atlanta. Should be good investment, says one guy who has a property there and kind of asking, but we say no, we are *fully funded.* Theodore's favorite reply because always people will be more interested if they can't get in, doesn't matter what.

But I'm thinking he doesn't know business like this. Better if I marry this friendly guy or something, we know that business!

But he has already with him a very nice smiling woman, young one he like to impress, so we are halfway there. We accept his card, and he repeat what strong interest he would have in partnership. He says he would care to offer a good faith money, if only we will send photograph of the place.

"Get back to me, soon as possible!" he calls. I think Theodore is getting too good, I tell him that, because even we have never seen the property which he has been putting out for sale. Gold dust is over us, *all over,* I say. Laughing and then kissing, I suggest to take a hotel room, pick up the stupid Buick tomorrow, or even next day, why not.

Richmond could be a rich town, we don't know state of Virginia but seem like gold mine already, we are thinking.

How can happiness be bad? It has to be good, like love. Do you think love can be evil? Probably it could cause lies. Or if it goes inside a bad person, it will come out evil, dirty like water from sewer pipe. But we are not bad, are we? Just happy.

I make up a little, some stories, when I want to show a quick explanation. I know that is not right, my habit to save time. Oh, it's not every day, but I make a few changes in small facts, I can admit. I don't tell Theodore everything in those days, but only if I spend some money which would seem more than I need, kind of unnecessary high number of dollars, maybe I reduce by one half. I could buy two bras, unusual expensive one like Lejaby or La Perla, and I bring one from the bag. Maybe I let the bag fall on the floor, like empty. Funny is he wouldn't care, not at all, but still I don't tell the real bill.

First, we lie to strangers, then to lovers, then to ourselves. Or must it be backward, start out with ourselves? Perhaps so, because of course we must stop truth in the heart, disregard that wish, or invent a new person who will be honest for us.

But one problem—it's no good to try to drop the new person later, because she stays on. Ready to help you next time when you have need to be honest. It's you, just another part—no, it won't be acting, it is really being. Her stories are yours, almost every one of them, and she loves what you love. Most of all, she loves the truth.

People start having conversation around here, you notice. We make music volume lower so everyone can hear, and I put a sign for book exchange shelf. Bring one, take one. No, it never will become library here, but we can show a concern for ideas.

Today, someone brought *New York Times*, so I will keep out one or two sections for the bookshelf. Maybe Arts, or even Education section. For the days after the club closes down and we all start walking into the future world. Some new topic to find out more, go somewhere ahead. Oh, I don't know, but better if they will learn anything. You know I have a big worry about young women. And we don't want to stay even as long as they want to dance in this place.

"How many bosses make you dance all night?" asks Katherine. "I never want to do any hard work if I can dance," she says.

"That will change," I say. "When you get my age, you might have another work you want to do, but it's late to get your experience. You cannot see that yet, but after the years go by, you will say, maybe, I wish I didn't hide so long dancing around in a dark club. My talent needs more light to develop." But she looks at me like I am kind of funny character who cannot know about her because I am dead probably soon.

Katherine laughs if I make changes in the club. You know, I don't want to keep the pole, because it is so normal to have a pole now. Why not put something else to dance around? Time to take it out when suburb ladies sign up in a pole-dancing class.

A ladder or a box of mirrors or a shower—I have a lot of ideas to avoid the so boring pole. A hammock! Even unicycle!

At least could be a tree, not a boring metal piece. Fashion pieces now are trees, in the Green Time.

Leo says, "Let's go to the forest, then. Close the club. Sell the building for manufacturing some crap of metal." I think he is serious, anyway about closing. I, too. But if he will finish this work, which had never interest for him except to know his brother a little more, I know he goes back to California and tries again with the music. And where am I?

In some forest, I suppose.

———

I came to America by sea, you know that, in last years of *Stefan Batory*. That was 1987, when I fell in love with Theodore. That ship had almost twenty years, just how I had, but it was ending in the time I was beginning. Theodore knew and he wanted always to cross over the Atlantic on the *Batory*, he said. *Battery*, actually he says. Everything he knows but he pronounce this name like for something in a radio, *battery*, which is so comical. Anyway, he made his trip to Europe because he knew it was to be soon the last voyage, just next year.

There is like a city of business, I remember because still I dream it, a butcher and bakery and salon and everything in the neighborhood, but floats on water. I think later that transfer is very good, because old life of mine goes all the way across together with me and Theodore to America, past into future, closed-up life into freedom life. And on the other side, I can let go that warm hand.

A lot of people never go home. It's not hard to forget it, most of the time. You can make the home story a little worse in your mind, adding dirt and taking out kisses, and you will be satisfied in your new country.

I don't belong here and can't really fit, but it's okay. If you live in New York, you probably will not be born there. But one day you could believe you are New Yorker, don't you think? So you are backward born, but unborn, even, if you refuse to belong.

Annette is soon going, speak of not belonging. She will take up full-time locksmith job, with her father in his business. Her certification is complete, and he says they can be equal partners now, so all the family is happy she will quit last hours dancing in the club. Leo want to write a speech for her retirement party. Everybody loves Annette, so we want to see the best of her life, but oh we will miss her! I hate to say goodbye, because I remember her from the first day I came here in the door. We look in our eyes, direct and smiling already, and I knew this could be a good place, even if not expected.

But now? Maybe we will not hire anyone else, and now Katherine dreams of going, too. Do you think they get inspiration and all leave here? Leo and I, like Mama and Papa at the door waving goodbye to the final one. I hope she can take off from the warm hand. Baby bird.

Javier and I don't sleep again together, but we meet to talk our secret talk. We laugh at the strange affair, daytime sneaking around at the mall or in a bad-smelling cafeteria at the hospital where we don't know any patient. There is so much to talk about, our mad theories of the world and stories, any perspective or idea to offer back and forward. We talk so fast, step over the other one usually, because we know we can't keep doing this, it's the most forbidden love and very soon we have to stop it. We can't be friends because how can we explain it, how we met and we know so much about the other, so everything would be on the back of lies.

But you never can forget a friend like that. We both were crying when we said this is the last day at our tragic cafeteria, and someone asks if we lost someone, thinking probably the surgery couldn't save him. But it has to save us. The love was only growing, so we took the worst surgery, to cut us apart.

"Your heart is in your eye," says Javier, his last words to me. Because I can't stop crying, and he knows that about me. Everything, he knows and loves it.

Is there any word for a friend in every way but sex is like a great lover of your life?

We always kept the Four Books, I and Theodore. As long as he will be professor, doing a possible research, there is no harm. We have the great novels near, to give importance for our work. Often at bedside in a hotel, we put the stack, and Theodore can read to me and make it home and safe. We really like the crooks in those books, but we are not the same.

Perhaps scholar-crook? No, I am just making a joke. Crook-scholar? Theodore says he is philanthropist, if on the road a stranger asks, because really this is our true work, to help other people to give up money. Charity is a spirit we put in, and no one can be sorry to have it, don't you think?

We don't say it, but we are escape artists, just need a little help some people getting out of life traps, to start a better one. Who will blame us? If someone would catch us, then we are just professor couple, sorry to mess up experiments some of the time but can't be perfect, anyone. Could be misunderstanding, you know probably is that, since the wife is foreign. Or foolishness, because nature of the professor is too far from criminal character, so funny he will even try that.

If I am worthy to go by that name Worthy, you can be. What do you want the world to know you for? Your answer should be big, showing great dreams. And now, how do you become worthy, not for every moment but for this moment? There you might need us, professionals in art of giving to become worthy.

If some people think you are worthy—for me, it's Daniel, Theodore, Leo, Javier, yes, few others—you keep it for building yourself, and it goes in your bones. And then nobody will see it, but you have ability to advance in your life like a military tank, even if you are dancing.

I don't want to hold back from you, since you offer to hear me many hours. My wish is you will carry this story *with* me—it will go in your bones, too—even after you hear all details of my worst. Why would you wait for anything else? It is easy to condemn, and I know you have found that everywhere, like I do.

Before we are gone, let us have a look at the trail we might leave. May I live on the earth, we don't ask before we are born, but we are here without asking and we could give something, be worthy, even if no mark will stay after.

Your heart holds what your eye doesn't see, until maybe in your dream you start to know what you missed or know what will come. I dreamed I told you everything but you were walking behind, and you tried to hear, but you couldn't. But you put your hand on me, and it was not to trap me, only touch.

There are no strangers, not really, in a dream. You put each one there because you know something about him. I think Theodore and I try to make our life like a dream, put people in for symbolic purpose. Theodore's folding theater, you know. We got lost there, making dream stories.

From Richmond to Atlanta is our best days. Some of the time I am driving, without license, and Theodore is reading from Four Books. He opens up anywhere and reads for ten minutes, then shuffle all the books and opens, and reads, and we keep on for hours, until night, when he begin to fear of my driving. He is drinking, not me, but I like usually to go very fast with all windows lowered, as I remember when I was a girl, and we didn't have air conditioner in such old car.

It's really crazy, sometimes bugs in the air heavy like rain on the way south. I think our good life will start again, after gray springtime of New York has chilled our love.

Once we stop for Theodore to call Steve, but we don't get an answer. We can surprise him, we suppose, just walking in his club! Theodore is quite excited, as I never saw him, like a boy he is laughing. He wants to go over that night, but we find a hotel first and then I beg him let's get sleep tonight and drive in there tomorrow, when his club probably will be quiet and we can say a good hello to Steve. That's good, when he says okay, because of course I hope I am looking better after bath and so on in the morning.

When I look in the mirror, I am seeing my grandfather around my cheeks and my old auntie below my eyes. All the faces I cannot run away from and they keep watching me, asking why I am here, wherever I travel. I turn off that light because they will start my worry, and I only want to wake up more pretty for Theodore to show his good friend. That night I was so young, but I didn't know.

On the next morning we ask about this postcard address, which the hotel manager seem not to want to know. But at last he does recognize, and after coffee we go to look for Steve, now I don't remember which street has those bars but I believe was in south. It isn't terrible part but we are watching around, and we find the door of Mexico City is closed, with no sign about what are the hours.

Let's have lunch, says Theodore. And we go, and then go back and still nobody, so Theodore says, let's have dinner. We have dinner. We go next door later, that one is open, and there we meet Barbara Blank.

Theodore is tall and I am little tall, so we look down to her beautiful face. It's not common because her eyes are close in between, like another Barbara, the singer Streisand. And her voice attract us, so deep!

"We don't see him for a couple days," she says about Steve. "But stay around, he'll be turning up. Have a drink?" And we like to. Live music soon will start, and Barbara is the singer, so there is no problem, no hurry.

Theodore remark about her original sound, beside some standard and new jazz. It's a wonderful night. We stay late. But Steve is never coming, so we return again and again. We expect he is on a trip, but Barbara has told us he usually will tell her. She doesn't know, but she invite us to stay at her place, if we would like to stay until he is back, is okay, we are friends.

So why not, as the best always on the road is a new friend. We go over to her house after checkout, so nice there is small extra room for us, and we say, just a couple of nights here and if he doesn't come back, then we move along.

We call but even there is no answer machine in his club. He just gets started, Barbara says, and then he takes off without put up any sign for a customer! Seem to be an interesting guy, she remark, but who knows. He is quiet and doesn't hire except one guy, and we hear Steve let him go last week or so, or maybe give a vacation. Actually we don't know.

Theodore walks around the back, and every day he is looking at a window back there. He can get in, he says. But I tell him don't be crazy, he is not in there.

"I know he is not there," he says, "but I can find out where he went, maybe. There could be a note by the phone." He really could be crazy, my husband, I am thinking.

I know, this is long story, but please, it is important to tell now. I know the club is hot today, global warming or something, not a *sexy* hot. Oh, god, bad for business if everyone in Tampa is stripping, then nobody will pay here inside!

Nobody will come in now, it's late, so let us talk. Please stay, because here is the terrible story you want to hear.

Might be they cut off power. I don't know if Leo has paid. Oh, but we have electricity, there is the fan working. Let's go by the fan, here, it's very cool in the wind. But keep on the light, a little light and you can see me, you will know Worthy doesn't lie.

Okay, you have a wine with me. Okay. That day I am supposed to fly back to New York, because Miguel has told me I can't wait, and I must destroy the false papers, most for me but also for him.

If we have ever any trouble, those papers from the wedding make everything worse, he says. Don't be sentimental, Miguel says. Why you didn't burn them the first day off the *QE2?* That's very serious, so he says I have to fly back. I don't agree anyone will find them at our professor-style apartment, but he offer to pay my ticket, so I know he couldn't be kidding, not at all.

Theodore doesn't need to go, too, but I think he will break in there. I ask him please to come, let's just go home. We get the car later, anyway that Buick is shit, we can leave it.

I am not sentimental, but Theodore is. He must see his old friend, now absolutely he cannot go before he could find out about Steve. Perhaps, he says, something is not as usual around here. I know this about him, and for sure if he has idea of anything wrong, it will magnify.

I am going to be on the plane thinking about this back window he wants to climb in? I am going to have to leave him in Barbara's house alone, with her? Just two?

Climb in there, also?

Theodore, we know, can be blue, very blue. He has obsession which can grow from mystery or waiting without resolution, and darkness get too much for him. He will be soon lost. And he might reach around then and find smiling Barbara. Or he could make one stupid decision to get in the window. Or both.

I consider to tell him I will go, but don't go. Stay instead at a hotel and become a spy, like my father. Yes, he was that, too, and probably not spy for the good guys, but I won't talk about him tonight. But how can I spy inside Barbara's house or at night outside the dark club? Oh, I'm getting crazy like Theodore. I am turning bad, soon to be a factory of false stories. I have to take the flight, I know it.

I will hope for the best. I don't deserve, because of Javier, for Theodore to keep trust, not betray me. We were happy on the road, but now I wonder if we have strength left for any future. The bonds of our marriage get weak. We each have been breaking down, like the shit Buick that looks good but has rust-out engine. As I go to the airport, I am singing an old days song from Joni Mitchell, *Old bonds are breaking down, love is gone! Ooh hoo, love is gone…*

I try quick as possible to turn my mind to New York. I will go shopping right after I burn the papers—actually cut up very small with scissors and throw away different places—and I will buy every dress and beautiful shoes I need, to bring Theodore back from Atlanta. I know she will get him, but I will get her. No fear. In three days I will be back, and without mercy. Is it love? It seem to be crisis, perhaps crisis of love.

I almost forget to say goodbye, since already in my mind I am coming back. I don't think Theodore has a plan to cheat, not at all, and he is kindly saying thank you for traveling to New York to protect our future. I won't go in Steve's club, he says, don't worry. But I don't feel confidence, instead deep fear of bad things coming. I can't explain, but could be like superstition, even I don't believe that.

I think we earn a turn for worse, and it is not something about luck. Try to have good judgment, I say to him. We have to work on that, my love, okay? Or we can be judged. I tell him I include myself, and he looks at me, I think surprised. Maybe that was a mistake, because then it begins to enter his mind I have done wrong but didn't tell him. We are split apart.

Still we kiss at the airport drop. I go on a weak point, I feel it, but they call me to board the plane. In that moment, I start to understand how much I could do only because with Theodore. False defense you have when you are two. I took off my coat in a snowstorm, exactly, that is the shock in my body. I never was brave, just think I was.

But why did I find courage if Theodore just is there to carry my ticket? He cannot fix everything, but he takes away my fear when he is beside me. More like valium than real protection is a man, you know.

The first time I care about a place is this crazy club. I never before paint a wall or want to buy a sofa to decorate a home. I don't know why here—yes, it is sudden mystery, because I don't believe it and still I do it. In New York, Theodore and his first wife made their place all right, but never for me is specially comfortable. But I don't change anything there, and this first time to go alone, I mostly just get out of there, my reflex to fly. Is all strange without Theodore, and I spend those New York days in the store getting my beautiful clothes.

So I don't get a phone call. I don't notice a light on the answer machine till it was next morning, when already the phone is ringing.

Police! They have Theodore *in custody*, which shock me so I can't ever forget the words. I know what it is, but I say nothing, only ask if he is okay. They say charges are breaking and entering, attempt burglary of a business, something like that, and I know what it is. He can go out on a bail, so if I come with that cash, he can be free.

I already reserve my flight, but it's evening, so I find out where to go the next morning to get him, and I expect to stay at the home of Barbara. This will be the second night of Theodore in the cell.

Some reason I can't call Barbara, not now, maybe later. I feel angry she didn't stop him. Maybe she has even help him. Why she didn't call me? I keep crying and walking round and round the apartment. I wish Mrs. Finch would be next door, and that cause me harder crying. Oh, if we can sit on the old couch together and I can hold those little hand bones, always cold, and she could tell me Theodore will be all right.

He fixes this, she would say. He fixes everything.

———

When I get off the plane that night, I have to finally call up Barbara. She says she was trying to contact me—is she lying?—because she must tell me worse news. Steve is reported missing several days ago, and they will hold Theodore there to do more questioning, in case he is guilty suspect in a crime of violence, too. They don't know what he was entering for in that club, and it's very suspicious now when Steve cannot be found. She is asking me when I know he saw Steve last time, and I wonder if she suspect him of murder or something. Possibly she help the police to get that idea?

Can you imagine how I am feeling? I don't know any law, or anything to do about all this trouble. I know just that I must see Theodore and help him, or better, have him help me to help him! I don't want at all to go to Barbara's, but I can't think of any idea to tell her that I must be in a hotel. Also, she knows more and maybe she will help me, if I make her believe Theodore is innocent, anyway of a murder charge. That is so crazy, of course, but it's true she does not know him for even a little more than one week.

You see my hand is shaking, look.

Have you feared someone you love? Were you stepping back to imagine, because maybe you have been too close up to him and couldn't see? All the time you thought one thing, and that was wrong. And worse even is to contemplate if nobody can know that person hiding. *Oh, god, who is Theodore?* But I don't let free my thoughts.

I have to get there, nothing else, that's it. I better not drive to the police without license, so I go by a taxi.

When I see Theodore, of course I know it is him, but for sure he has age about twenty years. He has his own clothes, with wrinkles all over, but I expect a prison suit, so this is better. If I cry I know I can't stop.

"Here's your man, ma'am," the guard says. I am hearing *Here's your madman.*

I feel only anger, no sympathy, but I try to show love, if I can find any. What I notice is his shame, maybe I never saw before, so I am more lost.

I see other women, even younger, maybe a daughter, who must come to this worst place to try to help a man, also *their madman*. Nobody knows how, but some know from before and they will know more for the next time how you talk to law, walk slowly, and smile only with cheeks. Careful not to show teeth like a dog.

But I forget to tell you about Barbara, night before when I arrive. I look into her beautiful eyes for any secret, constant so I don't hear anything she is saying. She gives me a paper with numbers to call, information about a bail and lawyers, etcetera, and that is very, very good, because I am so scared and tired. I believe she is sorry we came into her club, and I tell her I regret and thank you to help us so much we can't ever forget. I know we will have to talk, but I say please better let me go straight away to bed.

Maybe tomorrow we finish, my friend, because I have now to sleep, just as that night I am so tired that I lose my words. If you forgive to stop now, because I discover again too much.

I never in those days met Steve, but I have met his mother, Gloria. And the mother knew Theodore when they were young friends smoking up her house. Gloria was good person, and she was trying to find her son, but still she has concern for Theodore when her missing person paperwork is turning up him and not a killer. And nothing can be found, not where he lives when the mother goes there. They always were talking on the phone. Seem to be very strange disappearance.

She told police Theodore has to be innocent and please drop the charges, but isn't possible. Theodore doesn't help himself, and he doesn't let anyone else.

Also Clamence, you know already this character, in the book of Camus, will never walk over a bridge, because he didn't go back one night to help a girl who falls over. I know Theodore refuse to do something that will cause a second problem. He must be thinking about the Four Books, and become stubborn, and somewhere, somewhere the key is in the books. What he is thinking to do, like one of those characters?

Each one of them fools himself, but doesn't care.

I know he goes to these characters of Melville, Mann, Camus, and Nabokov. He is asking what should he do to escape out of this trap. He is in a corner, doesn't want to make a mistake. Good memory he has, perfect memory of all scenes, like a catalogue he goes through. Most of everything, he wouldn't like to be idiot like Hermann, in novel *Despair*, who by himself makes his terrible fate, by vanity. But maybe in this time he has forgot, which I don't ever, that also Hermann would not change his plan, which he loves too much, even when all evidence will show it doesn't work.

Theodore is quiet, thinking about where could he discover a key, I am sure. But I want him to help me, to talk to me. He looks down or even up, to the ceiling. I don't like to see them watch Theodore, the people around him.

They believe he is crazy.

He says always the same thing to me: "Don't stay around here. Go on. You don't know everything." Doesn't sound like him, it's nonsense for me.

"What happened?" I ask him. Maybe when they arrest him or he sits all night in a jail cell? I keep asking. I must do something or situation becomes more serious. They could take him to hospital, says Steve's mother, book him up there. Observation to find out what is going on, could he be really crazy?

Of course, I believe not. He is still in his folding theater. Of course he is not normal, but no, not crazy.

"Please, Theodore, don't hide from me. You know I can understand. Come out, I will help."

And then I get an idea. If I am crazy with him, maybe a chance he will hear me.

"I will get a gun," I say, "and come back here to get you free and we will return to Xalapa. Tonight." And then he quickly turn, and I'm sure he was winking. For one second, I believe it is true, we can have our adventure, as in a film.

We are not desperate in trouble, totally apart.

"Oh, please remember Clamence at the end of *The Fall*," I am begging. "He wants to have a chance to go back to the bridge. To save her and also himself. Please save us, both of us, Theodore!" But he doesn't wink again.

Now I see Leo wants me to come over there, and I know he is telling me time to stop talking to you. I shouldn't cry over the past, he says every day. We can have tears about today, if we like, but for yesterday it doesn't help, especially not.

But yesterday and today it's all mix of past life. Coming and going, I am. Just me, no monster.

I have to say more, before we stop for this night, just until Leo can forget it and go back to music. I have to say that I don't forget the wink, and that wink is like some spill of oil that is starting to light a small flame that doesn't go out, only gets bigger. I see in my mind his crazy blue eye, and then I see the whole face, need of shave, and everything is wrong there.

Wrong for us, and for me.

Nobody is talking about a bail anymore, not Theodore, not the lawyer we found from a friend of Gloria, not me. They are talking about a transfer to psychiatric facility, outside town, but they will let me visit after he settles. I imagine Theodore is expecting this will solve his case, and perhaps the lawyer too, but I have no words, only that flame that is glowing higher through my mind, to open the roof until the sky is clear.

I feel my years, even they are few. I am an old kid at this time, and I believe I carry more wisdom than these other ones who knows best as they are certified persons in any profession.

Okay, now I really must go to talk to Leo. Brush down his fur, all standing up, what a nice man! Many things he prefer not to know.

You cannot make out of old cake a new cake, but I believe Theodore has been thinking out of Four Books he can do it, fit together a new literature of his life. Or make the life so beautiful, living by the books he loves. A living book, and singing along with fantastic music, the story of our life in a very important fight against boredom and everything with stupid reason to get in our way.

That art of confidence is becoming to seem like magic to him, maybe for us both, now crazy mess or something, but worth to save. Who knows what we will believe next?

I am trying to follow him, stay in his world, but I lose when I find something in the house of Barbara. In the bedroom. I shouldn't look there, but I see on the floor a blue piece I recognize, under her bureau, from the hall when I am passing. And she is gone to the store, so I enter it and take out the undershorts of Theodore there. Of course only one explanation could be possible. And you don't leave it if you go there only once, so I know probably it was all the three nights when I have been in New York.

I know how he toss on the floor all his clothes, but don't believe where I found it. Same blue flower undershorts I bought for him in

Corsica, I stick back under the bureau. But I fold it perfect, so she will know when next time she cleans her house up, a woman was there after and has put a message for her.

Should I visit Theodore? What do you think? Do you think I have gone the good wife? Or have I gone the crazy wife?

I pack up and call about a hotel nearest by the facility and then a taxi. Barbara return as the taxi same moment arrives. She says no, no, but we will go together and why I have the suitcase—she knows and I know, but we are acting in the folding theater—and I wave, *bye-bye, thank you, don't worry, I will call.*

One thing about Theodore you should understand is bad case of claustrophobia. If you have human compassion, you must feel pity for people who has intense fear. This is why I don't understand he won't cooperate and get free, and I keep thinking, really he *has* gone mad, perhaps for that pressure. One time I was only playing to keep him in the closet, just press against for one second, and he already went absolutely full panic.

But he was winking at me, after what he did. Doesn't help me, only winks.

And this time I visit, he turns his back. I am wearing fabulous many-layer skirt I bought from New York boutique, to be strong, with his white straw hat from Mérida also. And after he looks, he pulls his pants up like irritated, again turns the back. And you know? I turn, too, and I go, and don't return for two days.

But keeps coming in my mind the way he pulls on his pants, and I think he should have his belt, and maybe he left it. I still have those feelings of a wife, but also having so much pain from thinking about Barbara with him.

I can't imagine he did it. I wonder did she ask him or only touch softly his knee or come over nude to his bed? Because I will not believe he went to *her* bed. But more I imagine, more I see that. He is going over there, down the hall, and he looks in, and she is in the bed reading, *one of the Four Books!* And he steps in, and she says, I was waiting, I knew you would come. They begin laughing, he is hugging her now in the bed, they are rolling—oh god, like the worst film in the wide world, I hate it. I hate them, but more I hate Theodore.

And also, it's true so I will say it, I feel insult from going in the new clothes for nothing. Always Theodore would say I am worthy of every man's eye, but now not even his eye is looking, and I am more alone, like orphan, isolate from all connection. My love has for me only a wink, a broken glance, and that I waited for in my pretty dresses.

He can go to hell, for what I care. He can just go! I stamp around, and I throw some things in the hotel, and they complain next door, pound on the wall.

Yes, I know I behave terrible. I have forgotten to love him, now in crisis, because I want him to love me in my beautiful fashions I don't need. What was happening to me? Am I only mad from jealousy, or have I change because our life, that life following Theodore, is poison for us?

What excuse can I choose, when I now look back?

Next time I go there he is catatonic, they explain to me. Or maybe sick, they don't know, could be fever of the brain. They take a test which has to come back with result. He is sleeping, so they allow few minutes only sitting by his bed, and a guard stays there. But I take off my belt, actually it is his one wrapped over, and I put it fast under his sheet so he will find it, because they said bring nothing there. I don't want for him to be dropping his pants, and that loses his hope.

I think love will not mix always with air, and it will flow out like a water pipe with air in that, and it seems like coughing out.

Pneumonia love. I had that with Theodore now, the love that still was there but not flowing out very good, sometimes not at all. And worse was I didn't know that, when it was only air coming.

So when I leave the belt, I feel completely it is for the dignity of Theodore.

I concentrate to do what small good I can do, so fear will not be the strongest, and I will avoid to throw more shoes in the hotel. I remember what advice Miguel and Daniel gave me, to smile and open my arms out with shoulders back when I am really afraid, because it goes right away then. Like that! Breath comes back, with power to do anything you need, and it was true.

I went to a hairdresser salon that day, just stop in there and ask for a new color and short in the front. Came out not very good, I thought so, but a man in the hotel had very bright eyes looking over me. I was in the bar for a wine, and he wanted to buy that drink.

"What a beautiful color is your hair," he says. "You don't see that light red color, very good you keep it natural." I remember that still, because I believe he tries to find something out about me. Is he watching me, the wife of Theodore, sent from the police?

I believe it looks like a ladybug, totally false, because the hair is still also dark, with some red patches. Can be typical ignorance for men, but no, this one is trying really too hard. I don't want him to pay, but he did it and then he expect to take me upstairs! Of course I say no, but he pushes. And maybe he has thought I work around that hotel, even for sex, I begin to understand that.

I always had Theodore like a bodyguard, but that night begins the rest of my life without. I can't suddenly alone manage the world so fast, even if inside my heart I am the Old Kid. But I do a smart thing, and I stay out in public eye even I am so tired I like to go up to my room and immediately sleep. Maybe he would rape me in a hotel basement, I don't know, or interrogate me about crimes, I don't know anymore what is going on. Only when I watch his car drive away, I finally leave the bar.

We are having a marriage breakdown, I and Theodore, double breakdown. One for two and each one alone in a nightmare.

I have itching under my skin, very deep. I stand in hot shower, and then I scratch my arms, those are the worst, and across the chest up to my neck. Back to hot shower. I sleep very little, and I worry about Theodore, wonder if he can sleep. Such a lot of noise there in his prison hospital, like a place for business all around the clock, I noticed. And light, which will make you crazy when you can't put it off. I imagine he is telling all the stories of our life under a big light, from some detective films I know that.

I sharply remember everything of that day and the next one. I don't deserve it to go away, that terrible memory from losing Theodore.

But I want to keep him, so I keep us on that day before. Just another glass wine. We look like a good pair, in the photos I have. Best is in the Mérida hats, and holding on to shoulders of each other and also hats, in the wind, and absolutely joy is overcoming us.

Assisting in suicide is a charge on me, same moment when I learn that Theodore is dead. Actually, no, I think they request to question me because he has died, and I am so shocked, I don't know what they could be saying, even about Theodore. I think must be his fever they spoke about, but isn't that. I am widow at this moment, but they would like me to go to the station for questions! I insist to go to see Theodore, and finally police offer to pick up and drive me there.

I don't want to describe him, so I am not going to do that, but you will know why I have scream if I tell you he has hang himself. I don't want to look anymore, so I start to run, all crying and hair hanging down. But they stop me, without sympathy, and request I go immediately for questions about "my role," like I am in a theater, and for moment I think Theodore can't be gone if he is still making a folding theater.

But I know his game is up, and he didn't want to be a leftover.

I don't think yet about myself, my feelings, only what he is thinking. Because always it was a plan I was living inside that he made for us. I only wish to know what he would have in his mind for me now, but I am completely guessing.

"Why you brought a belt two days ago?" says officer.

I am afraid, so I say only, "Theodore's belt?"

"We know this is his belt, but wasn't before in the room because we don't allow that. We have to charge you for encouragement of suicide, a kind of murder, you know that, we believe." Something like that he says. And then I am angry.

"You don't have shame! This is my husband, lying dead over there! I took him the belt for his sad shape, for his dignity, so he'll be feeling better and can get up and walk around, to be himself again. Are you kidding you believe I killed him?"

I can't talk now, because still I cry to think about it.

Okay, a moment, I am okay.

Anyway, this is what happened. Now you know. They charge me, and I have to get help from anyone I know. Even back to Theodore's university, to get a proof he was having problems for many years and getting progressive. And you won't believe it, how nice is Morris, after all when I meet him. But yes, the guy has a gross sweater, I am sure.

And Steve is turning up, and he will help, he says, because his mother like me very much and is trusting me about the belt. Steve is so sorry, and I will tell you more about him.

You see, some won't believe it. And prosecutors says I was jealous of Barbara, and in anger I choose to kill Theodore, or give him that idea of putting end to his life, with a tool I brought to do it. And says I have time it perfect so he will be most afraid and hopeless, which I have also encourage.

But I hope you will have confidence in me. I am true, but you know I feel guilty, but not for that reasons. For forgetting my love for him in those days before, first when I sleep around, even just once with Javier, and then to be without enough care that I don't make sure he is not becoming crazy. I believe I hold Theodore's madness back, until then, with power of love.

I hear Claudine Longet singing, and I imagine how she is, total serenity, and that helps me. We are in a bond together, because it is very easy to judge a woman, and without knowing her heart, you think she is a killer. Also because, yes, there is a happy part of the story which also Claudine knows, a love story. She lives still, I believe, with the lawyer for defense, and maybe they married and stayed living in Mexico. Mine is not lasting—I can tell you about him later—but that's okay, is perhaps my style.

Theodore lives for me, my pocket husband I draw out and put on a table for the weak times. My *madman*, what so many think, wasn't bad at all for me. He has strength to climb on a highest path, to make his miracle. To be in love, you don't have to be crazy, because you will later go crazy, anyway, for having it or not having it, but we got ours right away and never let go. We learn from start to stay far from boring, but you never know, even us could have turned into Mr. and Mrs. Bluelight, over at KMart all the time to pick up the deal. This was a joke of Theodore, but even now it's in the past, and no one heard of that special sale.

So long time ago. I know, I finally tell the story.

I still don't know which mistake was my worst one. If you know, please tell me, and I can avoid to repeat it.

————

PROFESSOR DIES IN SUICIDE PACT; WIFE CHARGED. You can find my
shocker story in old newspapers. Little story, not like Claudine on
television and so on.

They accuse Theodore, even when he is dead, and he would have
been hard laughing over that. Suicide, they told me, was not a crime
if it works, of course, because no one to charge with that crime.
But if you help someone, yes, can be a murder charge. The police,
or just one guy Bert—"only doing his job"—says Theodore was pre-
tended to be crazy and very sick with mental fever only so he can kill
himself. What? Yes, so we can kill him together! And then probably I
am supposed to kill myself, with some medicines Theodore told me
to keep, but I didn't. So they believe I am coward not to complete
this agreement on my side, and they don't have sympathy.

Or another says I left the belt because I was jealous of Barbara
and wanted to kill him. I knew he was very crazy and afraid when is
he locked up, and he was going to use it. I would try that, and they
never punish me because I am just stupid immigrant worried my
husband will be having his pants fall down. Disgrace for the village!

They believe we are confidence artists, and I will probably have
a scam, so maybe Theodore is telling to someone there in hospital
the tales about our travels on the road. Must be. I was so surprised,
because I don't know where they learn it, and I get afraid a little then.

He was very proud for all we pull over in those years, I know
that, and he would like to tell the world. He said that, "Just one
big pity we have to keep everything secret." He was so happy when
we work with Miguel or Daniel, because they can talk about some
strategy for hours to analyze why this is the wonderful trap for any
human. He was so ambitious those days, especially in Corsica he was
in his prime life, because there was no top on his boiling pot.

I think if he knew it will be soon over for him, he would like to
tell all the stories possible, even for just the nurse. Somebody work-

ing in that hospital knows more than you, most probably, but we
can't know who would it be. It's okay for me, because they believe
he is crazy and, if they even listen to details, they can't get any proof.

I know he was happy. He played his games until the last.

They dismiss it, at last, the charge on me. First the judge told me
I was wrong, and I would pay certainly in tears for that mistake. He
says everything over again about a violation of the rule not to bring
anything in that prison hospital. He couldn't absolutely understand
why I took his belt there, but it was not assisted suicide because I was
not there when Theodore decide to end his life and nobody can prove
any plan with me, even though, yes, I brought the belt.

"You know better, I am quite sure," judge says, and stop for air,
eyeing on me. "Only childrens doesn't know what signify a belt for
prisoners."

I respond I wore his belt sometimes because Theodore liked to
see how small looks my waist compared to him and that was sexy,
and the people in the court laughed a little. But I said I wanted my
husband I love very much to wear his belt again going out to the
world, walking with me up a great city avenue in the breeze, and then
even those men looked like tears in their eye.

Theodore would admire that for theater—I can hear *Bravo,
Lude!*—but it was true. I think so. This is how the life is, how truth is
getting made. Contrary ideas are coming together in one truth. We
have to always decide it.

Perhaps you still have a question or so to ask me in a while.

I am not running away anywhere, not this evening.

You wonder why I later go in business with Barbara, don't you? How
I went back after Montana to look for her in Atlanta? I could have
return to New York, and even look for Javier. Or fly to Mexico and
discover if Daniel could still love me. All those were choices, sure.

They are too unknown, and in that time I need to know. Barbara
I had discovered in her basic character. She will not sleep on a floor
for me, and I can never expect that.

Theodore told me my best friend is the enemy I know. I remember often some advice like that. It's hard, but you need to take it
serious. So I go to Barbara. And Theodore is there in Atlanta, where
they burned him. He didn't have transportation anymore, so I think
his spirit—could be he actually had one—stays around that town.
Anyway, it was that place I saw him last time. I missed him, because
he definitely was not in Montana, nowhere. Theodore could be in
darkness always, but never lacking his deep soul like piece of art he
makes over many years.

I believe we build a ghost. Sure, you can do that by adding pile of
memories in one place and concentrate about it. Why not? We own
the imagination, unless we rent it like a house to anyone else, and we
can use it for finding the loved ones, even spending time, even living
the life with them.

Of course, don't talk about it.

I don't live like a killer with bodies in back of the house garden.

People believe I am responsible, and there was anger from citi-
zens that didn't ever know me or Theodore, nothing from our life. So
I don't really care about that, but if I tell a whole story to one person,
that would be another case.

Please don't take me wrong because I speak like all this now is
from a closed book. I thought it was a dream! I still do that time
of year, in May, when starts to be hot a little at night in Tampa
and smells are changing to be more acid from the bodies around. I
can smell that and then comes back all the story in front of me. It
rains on me a sheet of goose skin. I see his clothes I gave to a beggar
man. I remember the fat man with oiled grey hair I took the Buick
to show him and he bought that. I hear my scraping voice when I

told bad news to Miguel on the telephone. I feel my stomach trying to eat stones.

I have now all Theodore's money—the last shirt, you know, has no pockets.

But where to go? That time I wanted to go far to south, but I couldn't go again to Key West, never. I only can think of one town in Florida, only that name. Key West, not a key for me. Not south but west!

There is my lawyer trying to give false comfort of sex. Not worth to tell. We have nothing to keep us. I must buy a ticket somewhere, so I decide California, San Diego. But I never arrive there, where the sky will be blue all the year, because I stop in Chicago. You know that I meet Larry, on a cloud over middle American land, and all below is corn and cows and I don't know. I wonder if I have gone all the way to West Coast, but you cannot know it. Maybe there, too, another Larry, another Mirek, the same long dead time, but outside more warm and bright than Montana. Maybe could be worse, I think.

I am a traveler, going new places at least in my heart. American style, I pick it up on the way. Leo says that, to let me know that he will understand if I go with someone who loves me. He does love, but without need coming from passion, and that kind of love either will last forever or will quit if there is a pressure, like moving over to California, if he will find someone to buy this club.

I am a traveler, I tell him, but also by the ground, on my feet. I want him to know I would like to go, if it goes that way. We don't figure it out yet.

But look who has come around here this afternoon—it is Jolie's little son! And he appears fat, or more fat. Still he needs the sunshine, doesn't he, but so good he can be coming around here again!

"Nicholas! You are big handsome cowboy now, so will you come over to me?" Oh, he is shy with Ludmila! He has kind of boots with his blue jeans, new ones, and remind me of out west. He looks pretty okay, but I think he was noticing we study like a book everything he does, and he just take a Coke and go back there to play music with Leo.

Drums are good for sick children, as you will guess.

Twenty dollars I will give him later. Every possibility I do if he comes, because he can give to his mother for keeping safe. I can't give to her, because you can't find the way how when you have a friend who needs. They don't want to take it, for shame. If you have some cash extra, more than you want to count anymore, it's so wonderful to give it, but how do you suggest that? If there is a kid, he can pass it from Auntie Ludie, and sometimes I put a note there also in his pocket. I write once that I really was dreaming to be a banker when I have that age of Nicholas, and even still I like to hand out money, and I will only be happy if she put it away for her son, because one like him, that luck I never get.

Robin Hood concept at that age has a great power, and I have kept a saving bank for the poor. Always I was counting out if there was more money from interest building inside, what my father told me about money growing in a bank, even I remember some idea that it grows faster all the time, I believe Theodore says this is *compounding*. I believe it will happen in my piggy also, so I keep opening up that bank from the bottom hole, counting over and over, and waiting until next day to try again so I can give my saving to any poor person and his family.

My father was laughing, and hasn't told me it isn't the same function with a small pig. Just the big one.

Now he would laugh more. And he would ask me what is the reason I don't work for the bank, if I like to pass out money and especially also take it when I shouldn't.

———

So what do you think about how long can I keep on here? It can't be so long before a cut flower will tilt over. I forever put a root, but not deep down.

In Atlanta, it's always more lovers, you know. But there is Steve, and his mother would like to get me for her lonely old boy, never married. Do you say spinster? Only for woman spinning alone? He spins before we are together, I am sure. Alone, as he was, I cannot imagine this man. One day he lost his car, if you can even believe it. On the next day he lost the keys. So he stops driving. And also Gloria is looking for a place with her son, to make family with us. Could be a safe feeling for me, because it's nearby to Theodore in a way.

Holding on. But to what? Only ideas, because the past is a broken-off piece with no link, just few smells and songs and pictures drifting in another room. No door there to open. Just a window and if you like to be Peeping Tom, if you please you go ahead, but I won't.

I like Steve very, very much for my best friend. He will be perfect to be a friend, but I can't love him. We need someone at the same moment, caring to give and also to get, but it couldn't be him for me. Sad to say, it was me for him, so we have to split off. I still today miss his funny heart and comical business plan. You know, that club never was really open, only for one week or so, then later a month or so after, one very busy weekend, then two months closed up—without any sign for the customers!

I'm singing soon, a beautiful song from Leo. We compose it in our morning robes, experiment some new lines. Wait till next week, you'll see, because our song will tell you a musical secret, and we make a cure for Nicholas. Leo studies about mystical subjects relate with notes, something like a certain harmonic tune he believes can rock around the universe. Leo is alchemist musician, this he tells me.

He calls me once melodious, and I was so sad and worry over that. Next time if he will call me harmonic, I told him that's good for me, and I am not mixed up with smelly. Isn't that for a bad odor, melodious? Leo used that word for a trucker arrive once in the club, I believe, because we were running all of us away from him. Oh god, in the whole bathroom. Poor Rebecca has to clean up in there, after. We didn't guess when he last showers, actually we consider to have one in the club after that.

Strip Spa, maybe that will go in California, if Leo will have a new location. Organic spa with, what about that, holistic stripping?

I am at intersection, what traffic headache always. A crossroad. You ask if I will track down my son, but that word—son—is not the right one. Mirek came down like meteor, I think, and set up his growing in my body, but he can't be a son from that. He goes beyond and beyond now, to any galaxy. Where I cannot exist if human life won't support there. You think I believe that?

No, I don't. But seems to me like science fiction story, maybe I say it before, so I haven't hope he will invite me to his home and offer normal chicken dinner on any day. Probably he will hate me, actually, and lock a door if I knock.

I think I have more concern whatever about Baryshnikov, if you really like to know. He also can't be kept inside, and he flies away, so I wonder why I love a bird but not the human who is doing that. I will think about that love question, why the bird can have understanding for this nature of flying but not the boy with similar wings from early on.

I didn't believe to baptize this boy, and the family of Larry insist for that. It's not because I don't feel religious or I carry anger about the church. Not for that, even those are true, but for longer history of my family. You will not know, perhaps, that to save Jewish babies during Holocaust, parents in some case giving their baby to a stranger, so that person arrange baptism for her and give her chance to live. Those few very brave ones, they are the true Christians, if you like to say that is best.

Not the mother of Larry, you must believe me, or his sister. Not Larry. Even if all of them was baptized once or many times.

Problem came after the war when those families kept the Jewish children, because the church doesn't want to lose that soul they put claim in the baptism. They didn't protect anymore, they steal for the church. In that name.

My mother could be a saved Jewish baby. I can't prove that, and she says no, that never happen. But probably they adopt her during the war, in 1943, her Catholic family, when she was newborn, few weeks, and they never admit any information about the birth. When she tried to discover that, there is something strange in a record, a blackout. She told me they never say more, only immediately she was baptize at a church, and they have the name and all documents.

But one time there came to our house a woman and man looking for her. They were Jewish, by the name we knew that, but I now don't even remember it. They left after talking a few minutes with my mother to ask about her parents, but they give up for some reason and said okay, could be we have a mistake in that file.

Maybe no one could find them again, if you try even.

My father was laughing and saying that will be the day your mother is Jewish. Not in this house, until they stand over my dead body.

We have dark hair and eyes, even my father, but my mother has the face of a pretty Jewish girl, in the old photos I see that. In her school they torment her, they say they know she is a Jew, not a child of the blond mother they saw in the market. But she always will deny it, and nobody can prove it.

If that is the truth, then I am Jewish, too! I don't mind, at least I don't have my blood from the Catholic Church. I think I came this way, from Jews who must give away their baby. I believe it. They saved my mother but should have give her back, because there is not any reward of doing what is right.

I was not baptized. My mother did not explain. My father wanted that, he told me many times, and I imagine what a fight over it, but I really don't know. I like to be Jewish, even without knowledge about it. I strongly know I don't want to baptize my son, if there is any chance I hand over his soul to them also.

But they force it, and Mirek goes there for baptism without me. I never saw it, but probably the soul went out there, going where they go, to bank of souls I suppose they like to count for gold.

Even if the boy is Jewish, like his mother, like the grandmother, they take his soul for the bank. Even in Heaven or even in Montana they can't tell that, like the boy can't tell it. You would like to believe if would be worth death, the Jewish soul is standing out, but is only a usual one.

Short before I am leaving Atlanta, I have big song and dance, over with Barbara and that crowd, but many more people. Some word about my crazy show is going out around the town, I guess. I prepare willow branches as my costume, with braid of vine and peach flowers or magnolia, too, and I don't know what more, everything of nature. Impossible dress, difficult to wear, which has to break open when I am dancing. Soon because hurts. Actually I had blood, pouring down, also on my feet where I danced. But I was singing okay, even so good they ask me to record in a studio one of these days. Normally the stripper will not sing, you know, so is a surprise and everyone is clapping I can't believe how long.

Of course, I fall in love that night, but didn't know yet it was handsome tall guy from Tampa coming up at once to congratulate this act. He wants to learn about when we are going down to Florida, perhaps very soon appearing nightly where he is living.

Maybe I have been a big star by now, I wonder, if I didn't travel away from Atlanta when I start to rise. Or at least a small star, I would be, above in the heavens.

There will be no answer for me, not anyway in words of truth I believed in when I met Theodore. But I must find a right one for you. Life cannot fit inside four or thousand or million books, but reasons for our life seem to add up in there, don't you think?

But reasons will run out, too. So life will pay back what we owe. Example is if you are not the man who took property from me and freedom of slave women of centuries past, still today I want all back from *you*. Sorry, but he is dead and you have a same look. I am still working for you, maybe, and I look for justice.

Not me, this is just example. I don't ask for your sacrifice.

I want to ask for hope, because I found out it is not nice to live without some of that, and of course kindness of a spirit, but if a breeze will not bring it, I don't know. You only can walk away from something if there *is* something.

When I travel away from Atlanta, I was burning up the world behind and I have the idea to open up a big new door. I will tell you something about how I make that, my strong card of love helping. I can't play a game so much now, than two years ago laughing when I light a fire of my life.

I don't run from Mirek, maybe you think that. Very slow walking, that's enough.

"Come early and stay forever," says Robert. "I already have arrange a few appearance for you in Tampa-St. Pete." He mention names, but I am not feeling risk about it, only say *whatever*.

There was sorrow to say goodbye to Steve and his mother over long dinner with two bottles wine. Steve says he will visit to hear me sing, so let him know, please. I notice he hasn't respect Robert so much, but you know, that's of course. Still all the best good luck, he offer, and also his mother. "But you anyway don't need it. Business grows in Florida all over like kudzu, so you can never stop a new talent down there."

Did Beatles say you can't hurry love?

It's not true. It was all in hurry, starting up and turning off. After few hours, driving and talking toward Tampa, our love was used. Little mind of Robert only storing handful ideas from website surfing, I suppose. Maybe accurate of that day, newsblast appear to give a latest answer, but never will be really true. We try to laugh, but we are bored. Then we hope to argue, maybe for drama, but hopeless case!

In Tampa, I like even less the idiotic friends of Robert we collect from Ybor, and we all pretend as far as can go, but nothing is true as Robert promised. Only palm trees around McDonald's.

I decide sooner than later, immediate getaway. At my age, you know how important will be very quick fix for mistakes you still can make. My travel bag sitting just on my feet, later from Atlanta I could ask for shipping all the rest, so I ask please to stop the car. Robert seem very angry for that, so I say only thank you when we approach the stoplight, and I just pop out.

I walk fast, and I see a quick place to enter, so they don't follow. If they look or not, I don't care. They don't find me.

Good, but problem is where I am, on East Highway 60 to Brandon. Not Champs-Élysées.

You could have your dreams like the great birds of Florida flying in the sun, but even in the night you won't be similar to Édith Piaf. Yes, she was in the bars, same as we live, but which street can be important.

I took a street where nobody lives yet or often stops by, really only is a highway. Not a high road, says Leo. Only career, also he says, would be used-car career on this highway, or some business like us here. Why his brother has start it, we could guess only. One or two people has comment to Leo they were so similar, but Leo never saw it. For many years they never talk until he died.

Family we mostly run away from, if we have any chance for that, and we try to choose better with few people we like. I don't understand why some doesn't let go, or want to build back a ruin, like Mirek.

He called up lately and was asking to speak to Ludmila.

At first when Leo has hand over the phone, I thought, oh, must be Larry, because the similar voice. I ask who is speaking.

"It's Mike," he answer. "Your son." Oh, god, I am thinking.

"Mirek?" I hesitate, because what to say?

"Your friend in Atlanta, Steve, told me your number where you work there. So I want just to make a contact so if I move down there to Florida or something, we will see each other." His voice is like a professional caller, completely like stranger for me.

"But we'll probably not be here longer," I say, "so that would be too late, I'm sure, because the club will be sold. And I don't have new address at this moment, but if you like to leave your telephone…" This is how I am talking, nothing is certain, too bad, etcetera.

"Mother," he says, "why don't you want to see me?"

"I am at my work right now, you know, and is quite busy, perhaps you can hear all around, so I will call if you want to in a next few days or so."

"Mother, I need your help now," he says. "I wish I haven't need to say that, Mom, but it's pretty serious situation for me, that I never cause, and…"

"Maybe your father or grandmother will be able to help, before I arrive at a new job," I answer, then move over the bar for more shouting background and music, some clap and clatter crazy place. But he doesn't stop, and over again he is calling me *Mother*, until *Ludmila* again. Like a friend, but—no, the voice is weighing down.

"I have to go right away," then I say. "Sorry, boss says it." And I hang it up. Maybe I said goodbye and good luck about it, or could be not, I don't know. But I was shaking, from terror. I think this boy, my son, is turn out worse than me. I sadly hope no one recognize our relation.

So now this happens, and Steve never probably learn it's not a help to me. He would like to assist, I know, and he would mean it very well.

All the time I think of Nicholas, Jolie's boy. I don't have to say more. That boy even would give back the money this afternoon from his pocket. "You need that, Auntie Ludie, for dresses!" he says. Maybe he intend for clothes for naked dancers, I think he has seen, even when Jolie took him back to the drums.

Or could be just love, because everything is love, his game of love. He always win it, our Nicholas. And then give back to the world some fancy feeling, you know, suddenly joy just from that small person of power.

I believe he could get well, with so much power, but this is only love speaking. Well, could be shouting or singing for us, and of course we are hoping that.

Justice doesn't come even for rats, Theodore like to say. *Just is*, he calls it. Like you say, *Whatever*.

But also he would say, "Chances are good, very good." And he means universe is tilt in that direction, so even with hardly justice on the earth, you may likely fall in hands of good, because *just is*.

I don't think he really was out of his mind most of his life, do you?

My condition is hope, but a little burned on edges. Still good.

One day perhaps I have chance to speak to Mirek in serious, and I will be able to tell him sorry I use him before he was born. He was my safety, when his father is angry and would like to beat me. I didn't care more, just that.

And I will confess it. I also use him for protection after, or that memory of him. If I am supposed to be weak, I can be also stronger, I find out. So one or two times, I escape some danger with that, even was a lie.

"Please, I am pregnant," I said. "Only last week I find it out."

I learn to lie in my body. "I am very sick, down there, believe me," I say, if some man doesn't know me at all and anyway never would have a concern about my baby.

I did one more confidence artwork soon after Theodore. He was in spirit with me. It was kind of gift for him, to let him help me one more final time and make a better memory for his widow he left here. I believe in him, so near in those days, like pushing for something. Each time I remember about him, he seem to be talking about a plan. My ideas receive direct out of his mind, I really believe. Perhaps I like to think that.

"Only take from a man," he remind me. "And create me, find me there in the man. Also remember I am also in the Four Books, and please be very good student."

Still I am angry sometimes, for my abandoning, and I don't want to listen. But I imagine his voice, I create my man back alive—why? To forget loneliness of widow life?

One day comes a call from guess who? Morris.

He checks up on me, he says, after one month. He likes to see I am everything okay, also to tell me about some surprise he has. I hear Morris is excited, some air trapping in the voice, approaching to laugh or shout. For him, I thought was strange.

"We have collect around the department for you, my dear, because you mention some bills to pay of Theodore. I have that fund... if you return to New York soon."

"Oh, goodness, I don't need!" I answer. "I will find a work soon in Atlanta, I am sure."

"No," says Morris. "We are expecting you will return to New York, don't you know? And we want to help, and even you can stay over by us...by me. If you don't want to be staying over in Theodore's place again yet."

At that moment I recognize it—the wolf is back! I recognize not all was false from Theodore. I decide is a good idea to make some profit for me, and part for Theodore, and perhaps some fun for both.

I tell him I will think and tell him soon, but also look about how to get there, maybe on the bus. Thank you, thank you, I repeat. I am acting a poor widow.

"Not on the Greyhound!" laugh Morris. "Let me send forward some portion of this fund first. I will research about how much by best cost airline, and this check I can let you receive by mail."

He is cheap gentleman, isn't he?

"Oh, really I don't feel bother to come to New York by the Greyhound Bus. Is okay," I am insisting, "I enjoy that ride." Theodore in back of my mind laughing says, *Give it all you got, baby!*

"I can prepare about two or three sandwiches," I am adding, "for those travel days."

"Promise you don't talk to a strange man," says Morris. He is easy on the hook, doesn't feel that yet. He chuckle or cackle, whatever you say, as manner to flirt, I believe. I only feel surprise because I am always smelling the sweater, even by telephone. Also I see a face skin hanging—this is coming off like a snake!

That dirty old wolf, he is sniffing out anything to eat. Even at last he said it: "I like to eat you, my dear Ludmila, you are very sweet."

So I have a good time in next few days. I mention my old coat I must take to cleaners to bring for January in New York, and he is too happy, so he speaks sooner, too fast.

"Would you need a new coat? Or like to have that, even? I could add to the check a hundred dollars, or maybe little more." But then he is worried to offer too much, and he says, "Or down there in Atlanta, probably less needed than New York." He can't figure up what is better, more money before or more waiting for me so I will come up there. It's so funny if you are watching a cheap guy try out playing millionaire, but who will be stretching few dollars all around the place in a big show.

"Oh, probably I don't need it. But true, I should look better, now I see how I am running down after all this troubles." Of course, he says impossible I could lose my beauty, because always I will have it until seventy years old, and then going on and on and over again, until adding fifty dollars more, and then some more.

Meantime I return to New York for selling the place there we had, only that, because I don't want to return to Theodore's remainders, or next-door apartment, now without Mrs. Finch long ago gone to blue sky and of course love of my life, now only that comic voice and, I want to say most this, all the good and love in my head or heart.

I wonder often if I had a chance to go again, if I would take the belt for Theodore, if I could save us. I don't know if I am innocent, here or there.

I took some walks around a Central Park never I remember that cold, and to our favorite old Chinese food restaurant, Dumplings, that was our name to remember. I told there so many lies about Theodore, so not to make them sad. *He took a trip for a prize in Paris. We are buying land so we have to live in Xalapa, but we always love it here also.*

One afternoon walking suddenly I look up and see there his university window. I'm counting up until the fifth floor, and I imagine to see Theodore, his hand waving.

I do see it, perhaps, because who will know if that picture is in my mind only?

And so I am just standing outside in a long blue coat Morris bought for me but he never knew that. I let him send everything—yes, it was whole check because finally he couldn't stop one more addition. You already know, not so big as Morris suggest. Post office has mail it to me in New York, so I don't have to see him, just make deposit immediately. And I am not able to answer that ringing and ringing phone down there in Atlanta—or when Morris one day will get idea to call in New York to check if service is maybe stopped. I still wonder if he will creep into our club in Tampa, looking with big eyes at Carmen and Bella! Poor guy missed out again all the dancing in life. Possibly Morris is in a grave anyway for few years now.

So you completely know what next came. At last you understand the future is in the past, if it will exist for good or bad judgment by someone you won't know. You would like protection against it, but you have it already if you know who you are.

Perhaps I am not person to say that, of course you laugh. But you expect someone soon comes along—quite beautiful and would love to help. And you understand the story if it goes on like in Theodore's folding theater. Can you imagine if some evening a heartstealer singer remind you the song or two you carry from me?

Here I just disappear, stop being anyone anymore.

Now is your turn to be anyone. There is no word more of Worthy, if you should ask.

acknowledgments

Thank you to my husband Don Morrill for his unwavering belief in this voice and his loving support through many years' writing. I am immensely grateful to all friends of Worthy, from first audiences at readings to those dear and devoted who asked after her as though she existed and would one day live between these covers. Thank you to the Virginia Center for the Creative Arts for the residency that made the difference, to Casa Libre en la Solana for the weeks that gave this book its start, to the Dana Foundation for funding over several summers, and to the Council on International Educational Exchange for the faculty seminar to Poland and Germany. Thank you to Michelle Dotter, my attentive editor, for kind assurance throughout the process. To all benefactors at Dzanc Books, beginning with Steve Gillis, my fullest appreciation.

about the author

Lisa Birnbaum's work in fiction, nonfiction, poetry, and spoken word performance has been supported by numerous grants and writers' residencies. Her writing has appeared in journals such as *Connecticut Review, Puerto del Sol, Quarter After Eight,* and *Kestrel.* She teaches writing and literature at the University of Tampa and lives in Tampa, FL.